Aaron's Dark Secret

by

Ann Bixby Herold

Cover Illustration by Joy Frailey

Aaron's Dark Secret
by
Ann Bixby Herold

To
Matt, Nancy, and Louise

Chapter One

The narrow street was packed with people. There seemed to be no way through the crowd. Aaron limped over to a patch of shade beneath a wall. He took the weight off his left leg and sighed with relief.

The crowd was so thick it was impossible to see what was going on. He hopped up onto a rock, and stretched as tall as he could, but he still couldn't see.

"There is a good view up here," a voice said.

Aaron looked up. He found himself staring at a pair of dusty sandaled feet. "From here you can see everything," the voice went on. "Come up. There is plenty of room."

A boy was sitting on the wall. His blue eyes stared down into Aaron's brown ones as he reached down a hand.

"Here," he said. "Let me help you."

Even with the boy's help, it was hard to climb the wall with only one good leg. Aaron gritted his teeth against the pain. He reached the top and lowered himself into a sitting position.

"Thank you," he gasped.

"I saw you coming," the boy said. "You lean on your staff like an old man."

The pain was easing and Aaron grinned.

"That's what my father said."

"How did you hurt your leg?" the boy asked.

"I twisted my ankle when I fell on a hillside," Aaron explained. "I couldn't walk at all at first, but it is getting better now."

"What is your name?" the boy asked.

"I am Aaron, son of Joseph."

"And I am Benjamin, also son of Joseph," the boy laughed. "Are we long lost brothers?"

"My father is a shepherd," Aaron told him.

"Mine is a fisherman," said Benjamin. "We live here in Capernaum. Where do you graze your sheep?"

"A good day's walk from here," Aaron answered. Benjamin asked a lot of questions, but it was nice to have someone his own age to talk to. "My village is. . . . ."

Shouts from the street below interrupted him.

"Make way! Make way for the sick."

Four men were trying to carry a small bed through the crowd. On the bed, partly covered by a blanket, lay a paralyzed man. Aaron and Benjamin could see the man clearly.

"I wonder where they are taking him," Aaron said.

Benjamin pointed down the street.

"To that house," he said. "The one where the crowd is thickest."

"What for?"

"To be healed by Jesus."

"Jesus?"

"Haven't you heard of Jesus of Nazareth?" Benjamin asked in amazement.

Aaron shook his head. "My father and I have only been in Capernaum two days," he said. "I have been on my own because my father is busy."

"Jesus of Nazareth is a teacher who heals the sick," Benjamin explained. "He works miracles."

"Miracles?" Aaron laughed. "I don't believe in such things."

"Neither did I," said Benjamin. "But then my mother's sister went to him. Her skin was covered with sores that itched and itched. My mother said she had been like that for years. No one would marry her. Nobody wanted to eat the meals she cooked. She was an outcast. But the disease left her as soon as the Rabbi touched her. Now her skin is just like anybody else's."

"How is that possible?" Aaron asked. "Did you see it happen?"

"No, but she said . . . . ."

"Maybe her skin got better by itself."

"It couldn't happen that quickly," Benjamin argued. "It was a miracle. Jesus has cured all kinds of sick people. Ask anybody."

"I still don't believe it."

"Look at this crowd, Aaron." Benjamin waved an impatient arm. "Do you think so many people would be here if it wasn't true? Some of my father's friends have given up everything to follow Jesus of Nazareth. They were fishermen too. They walked away from their boats, just like that. Simon Peter owned his own boat." Benjamin shook his head, as if he still couldn't believe it. "Do you know how hard you must work to own your own boat?"

"Make way!"

The two boys watched as the crowd parted to let the paralyzed man through. The bed swayed as his bearers shouldered people aside. Aaron thought the man would fall off and be trampled underfoot.

"They will never be able to get that man inside the house," Benjamin said. "There are too many people in there already."

"They will never reach the door," Aaron said.

Aaron was right. There were so many people clamoring to be let in the four men gave up.

"I told you!" he said in triumph.

The men eased the bed out of the crush of people. They put it down at the end of the house wall. They seemed to be arguing about what to do next. One man was pointing to an outside staircase leading to the roof of the house. The other men stared at the staircase. They argued backwards and forwards across the bed. Then, one by one, they nodded.

"What are they going to do with him now?" Benjamin wondered out loud.

"I think they are going to take him up to the roof," said Aaron.

"Whatever for?"

"I don't know. Maybe they want to put him somewhere out of the way and try again later."

They watched the men carry the bed up the stairs. Up on the roof the men put it down and walked around. They were pointing down at the tiles, as if choosing a spot.

At last they stopped pacing. Two of the men knelt down and started to remove the tiles. The third man tied the paralyzed man to his bed with the blanket. The fourth took down the rooftop clotheslines.

"They are making a hole in the roof!" Benjamin cried as the tiles were stacked to one side. "They are going to lower the man into the house so Jesus can cure him."

It seemed a waste of time to Aaron. "What if Jesus can't cure him?" he asked. "They will only have to haul him out again."

When the hole was big enough, the men carried the bed over. They tied the clotheslines to the corners. The bed tilted to one side just before it disappeared from sight.

Both Aaron and Benjamin gasped.

"I hope the ropes hold," Aaron said.

"And the blanket," said Benjamin. "I wish we were inside the house. Can you imagine the looks on people's faces when that bed comes sailing down out of the sky?"

They looked at each other and burst out laughing.

Many other people had seen the paralyzed man being lowered through the roof. Everyone waited impatiently for something to happen. Minutes passed. Still they waited. The crowd grew silent.

"What will the owner of the house say when he sees that big hole in his roof?" Aaron asked in a whisper.

"He won't mind," Benjamin said. "The man will be cured and that is all that matters."

Aaron looked at him and laughed. He was about to make a joke about the man from Nazareth using one more miracle to mend the roof, when the crowd stirred and a murmur arose from the people closest to the house.

The door was opening.

From where Aaron and Benjamin were sitting it was impossible to see who was coming out of the house. Aaron shaded his eyes as he strained to see. To his surprise his heart was beating faster. Benjamin made no effort to hide his excitement.

"Can you see anything?" he gasped.

"No. Wait. A bed. I can see part of a bed!" Aaron cried.

"I see it too."

They knew it was the same one, because of the ropes tied to the four corners. A man was carrying the bed on his shoulders. As the crowd moved back to let him out, they saw it was a man wrapped in a blanket. He stood on the doorstep and raised his face to the sky.

"Praise God!" he cried.

The crowd took up the cry. Hands reached out to touch him.

"He is cured!" Benjamin cried in triumph. He dug his elbow in Aaron's ribs.

"How do you know it is the same man?" Aaron asked.

"Of course it is."

Aaron strained to see. If only the sun wasn't so bright! He blinked and used both hands to shade his eyes. From a distance it certainly *looked* like the same man—a healthy looking version of the man on the bed. He couldn't believe it. Was it a trick? Was it the man's brother? Somebody dressed to look like him?

The crowd parted to let the man through.

Eager hands helped to steady the bed each time the man stopped to lift his head and cry "Praise God!" His friends echoed the words as they made their way after him.

"He is coming this way," Benjamin whispered.

As the man passed below the wall, Aaron leaned forward. He narrowed his eyes and carefully looked the man over.

"I suppose it is the same man," he said slowly. "It certainly looks like him."

"Of course it is," Benjamin said. "Now do you believe the Rabbi Jesus can work miracles?"

Aaron didn't answer him. He couldn't take his eyes from the scene in the street below. The man was walking without any help now. He stopped every so often to adjust the weight of the bed. It was the kind of thing a healthy man would do. Once free of the crowd, his friends caught up with him. Aaron could hear them trying to persuade him to let them carry the bed.

"I can carry it myself," the man's voice was firm and clear. "*He* told me to!"

Aaron watched him until he disappeared from sight. Benjamin was saying something, but Aaron didn't hear a word.

He still couldn't believe his eyes. How could a man be unable to walk one minute, and healthy enough to carry his own bed the next?

What had happened inside the house?

Who was this man called Jesus of Nazareth?

Chapter Two

When Aaron twisted his ankle, he never dreamed that the painful accident would be the cause of his first visit to Capernaum.

It had been a morning like any other. Aaron was out of bed at dawn. He and his younger brother were to take over the day watch on a hillside outside the village. Aaron was glad he was going to guard the flock with Mark. Mark was good company. He liked to tell stories. He loved to sing to the music Aaron played on his reed pipe. Sometimes the boys made up their own words and music.

A watch with Mark passed much more quickly than one with their older brother, John.

John was so serious about work. He watched the sheep and goats with eyes as sharp as an eagle. He expected his brothers to be on guard the whole time. It was no good Aaron explaining that all the times he and Mark had shared a watch, they had never lost an animal, or that there was nothing wrong with having some fun while you worked. John wouldn't understand.

"Work comes first," he always said. He talked endlessly about the flock. He worried about the vegetables they had planted, and the grain. Would there be enough to last them until the next harvest?

He is much worse than Father, Aaron thought.

Aaron's father was a good shepherd, but he wasn't a worrier. When it was quiet on a watch, he often told stories to while away the time. Sometimes he would tell Aaron to collect some stones and pick out a tree as a target. Then he would pull his sling from his belt and challenge Aaron to a competition. Father would put a stone in his sling. With a flick of his wrist, he would send the sling whirling around his head. When he let go of one of the strings and the stone flew out, it always hit the target.

Aaron could beat John and Mark, but he never could beat Father. When he got discouraged, Father would throw his arm around him and give him a hug.

"It takes years of practice, my son," he would say. "Don't give up. You will beat me yet."

And his great laugh would boom back from the green hillsides.

I'd rather watch the sheep with anybody but John, Aaron thought.

And so he didn't grumble much that morning when he had to get off his warm pallet on the sleeping platform. His pallet was a thin mattress stuffed with sheep's wool and covered by a goatskin quilt. Aaron rolled them both up and stacked them against the wall.

He was shivering with cold when he joined Mark in the doorway of their small one-roomed house. Outside it was a cold spring morning. Nothing stirred. The whole village seemed to be sleeping.

Everyone except us, Aaron thought with a sigh.

He tied the belt of his robe and bent over the bucket that stood by the door. The water was cold against his sleep-swollen face. It made him gasp.

"Are you hungry?" Mark mumbled through a mouthful of bread.

Aaron swallowed a yawn and nodded. Mark handed him a hunk of bread and a dipper of goat's milk from the clay pot on the shelf. Aaron drank and refilled the dipper twice.

When he was full, Aaron tucked his sling and his club into his belt and reached for his staff.

"Don't forget your pipe," Mark said.

"I have it."

"Go with God," Mother called softly from the darkest corner of the sleeping platform. She always woke up just as they were leaving. "I will send Mary to you with the midday meal."

Not everyone was asleep in the village. There were other flocks and other shepherds. Here and there a boy, eyes cloudy with sleep, stood yawning in a doorway. Aaron and Mark raised their hands in silent greeting as they passed by.

By the time they reached the hillside, they were both wide awake.

"There he is," Aaron said. John, wrapped in his cloak, was examining the flock penned in a fold in the hills. "After a long night's watch don't you think he would be tired? Or sleepy? Do you think he sat down at *all* during the night?"

Mark laughed. "He is serious about his work, Aaron," he said. "I think it is because he is the oldest. Maybe you would be the same if you were the first son instead of the second."

"Never," said Aaron. "I think sheep are stupid. I *hate* them. I wish the whole flock would run off and then Father would have to do some other kind of work. I wish we could live in Capernaum."

"Father is a shepherd and Capernaum is a town, Aaron," Mark said. "What would he do there? Without our flock how would we eat?" He shook his head. "John says you often speak without thinking."

Aaron loved Mark but sometimes he wanted to poke him with his staff to wake him up and make him understand.

"Never mind about John," he said in disgust. "What about you? Is this what you want to do with the rest of your life? Sit on a hillside and watch sheep?"

"Why not? It is a good life," Mark said. "What else would I do?"

Aaron put his pipe to his lips and blew a few sharp notes. It was no use talking to Mark.

At the sound of Aaron's pipe, John looked up and waved. When they reached him, he showed no sign of wanting to go home. Aaron couldn't understand it. After a cold lonely night watch he was always waiting impatiently for somebody to take over the flock so he could go home.

"Aren't you tired, John?" he asked. "Or hungry?"

"Of course I am," John answered. "But there is something I must tell you both before I leave."

He was worried about two of the lambs. He

pointed them out and said, "It would be best to keep them penned with their mothers today."

Aaron groaned under his breath. It meant he and Mark couldn't be together. One would have to guard the sick lambs while the other watched the rest of the flock. It would be a long boring day without Mark's cheerful company.

"Aren't you going to tell Father about the lambs?" he asked. "Surely it is his decision."

John's face flushed.

"Of course I will tell Father."

"You had better ask him to come and see them for himself," Aaron insisted.

"Of course I will. I know my duty," John frowned at him. "Meanwhile they are to be kept away from the rest of the flock. Is that understood, Aaron?"

Aaron nodded. When John turned away he winked at Mark, and Mark grinned back. They both knew their father would come straightaway. If the lambs were really sick, he would stay with them himself. If they weren't, they would be returned to the flock. Either way Mark and Aaron would soon be back together.

Aaron stayed with the lambs and their mothers while Mark took the rest of the flock into the hills. Father came within the hour.

"There seems to be nothing seriously wrong," he said after he had examined them. "John worries, but it is better to worry too much than too little."

They carried the lambs back to the flock. The lamb in Aaron's arms bleated for its mother. The mother baaed anxiously as she trotted along behind.

Aaron looked back at her. *How can anything as pretty as a lamb grow up to be a sheep?* he thought in disgust.

When they reached the brow of the hill, Aaron's father stopped.

"Look around you, Aaron." His deep voice boomed out over the valley. "Did God ever create a land more beautiful than this? Listen to the birds. Breathe the sweet air. To live here is to be the chosen of creation!"

Aaron looked out over the green hills and valleys. He never noticed the countryside unless it was pointed out to him. It was beautiful, he could see that, but it was empty.

Aaron liked people. Village life was more beautiful to him. To listen to the old men telling stories, the women gossiping at the well, that was life to Aaron. To meet a passing traveler with news of the outside world was an exciting event. However bright the day, however green the grass, the hillsides held no interest for him. They were empty and lonely, unless someone like Mark or Father was there.

When their father had gone home, the two boys decided to celebrate their change in luck with some music. Aaron played his pipe and Mark sang at the top of his voice. They leaped in and out and over the rocks. The nearest sheep watched them in stupid wonder.

When Mary came with a basket of food, Aaron piped her up the hill.

Mary laughed and skipped in time to the music. Mary was the youngest child. Her brothers loved her dearly. And so, when she said, "I cannot stay, Mother has work for me," Aaron followed her halfway down the hill, playing her favorite tune.

It was lucky he did. As she ran homeward, a wild dog appeared from behind a rock. It saw Mary and bared its teeth.

When Mary started to run, the dog chased her. Her scream was all her brothers needed. Like hares, they bounded to her rescue.

Aaron was the closest. He saw the look of terror on her face. He flew down the rock-strewn hillside. He shouted at the top of his lungs and waved his club.

Mary reached a tree and dodged behind it. The dog circled the tree, snapping and snarling. It was closing in, and Mary screamed again.

Aaron leaped up onto a flat-topped rock that overhung the tree. He could hear Mark somewhere behind him. As he got ready to jump, Mark shouted, "Duck, Aaron!" A stone whistled past Aaron's ear. It missed the dog by less than a hand's length.

Aaron swung his club around his head and launched himself off the rock. The dog had been frightened by Mark's stone. It was terrified by the roar that came from Aaron. It turned and ran.

Aaron landed on a pile of loose stones. As his body hurtled forward, his foot caught in a hole. He tried to regain his balance and felt a sharp pain in his left ankle.

By the time Mary and Mark reached him, his ankle was already swollen to twice its normal size. When he tried to stand, daggers of pain shot up his leg.

Mark calmed a weeping Mary, and sent her home for help. "Ask Father or John to come," he said. "Someone must carry Aaron home and I can't leave the sheep.

John came striding over the hills, his robe flapping around his long legs. He was nearly as tall as Father and strong enough to carry Aaron on his back. The journey home was agony for Aaron. John was angry and made no effort to walk carefully. He seemed to think the wild dog was a story and nothing more.

"Playing, no doubt," he muttered. "Acting like children when there is work to be done. Of you and Mark, you are the worst, Aaron, for you are older and should know better."

Aaron, draped across John's shoulders like a dead sheep, gasped at each jolt. He clenched his fists against the pain and his mounting anger. John was always so ready to believe the worst!

He had more luck with Father. Mary had already told her story by the time they arrived home. Father showed no sign of doubting it.

"You were injured in a good cause, Aaron," he said. "I pray to God that your leg is not broken."

"How can you tell if it is?" Mary asked.

"We will have to wait until the swelling goes down," Mother told her. "Put him down here, John, on the bench outside the door, and I will bathe it."

She sent Aaron's older sister Rachel to the well for cool fresh water. Aaron sat in the sun with his leg propped up. It didn't hurt too much as long as he kept it still.

It was days before the swelling went down. When his ankle looked better, he tried to stand on it, but the pain shot up his leg. He tried hopping on one foot, but that jarred his bad leg. He used his staff as a crutch, but it wasn't much help. The only painless way to get around was in a sitting position, with his left leg lifted off the ground. As long as he didn't knock it, it hardly hurt at all.

Because he couldn't walk, Aaron had to stay at home. John and Mark, and sometimes Rachel, had to do his share of the work as well as their own. It was a busy time of the year. There were the sheep and goats to watch, the early wheat and barley to harvest, and the plots of young vegetables to till. Each row of plants had to be watered every day and weeded. It was an endless task.

"Your accident couldn't have happened at a worse time," Mother sighed. "Your father has to take the winter fleeces to Capernaum to sell. There will be even more work while he is gone."

"When is he going?" Aaron asked.

"In a day or so. I hope your ankle will be better by then."

Aaron's leg looked better, but he still complained of pain. He talked about it so much his mother and grandmother were worried. Grandmother lived with them. She was almost blind. A strange milky film covered her eyes. She spent most of her day sitting in the sun, working at simple tasks. She enjoyed having Aaron home and she spoiled him.

"I have bathed his ankle time and again," she said. "I have rubbed oil into the skin. Surely it should be better by now?"

"It should," Mother agreed. "I don't understand it. If the bone had snapped, we would be able to feel it."

John had an idea why Aaron's ankle wasn't getting better. "I don't believe it hurts as much as Aaron says," he told Mark and Rachel. "He doesn't want to go back to work. He is always complaining about the sheep. What better way to get out of watching them than by saying you can't walk? How will he chase them if they stray? How will he ward off the wild animals that prey on them?"

Rachel agreed with John. Even good-natured Mark was beginning to wonder, but when John said he was going to talk to Father, Mark said, "Give Aaron another day or two, John. After all, he did hurt himself saving Mary." And so John kept silent.

John had guessed the truth, although Aaron would never admit it. He was enjoying himself in the village. He had decided to make his escape from work last as long as possible.

Chapter Three

Because of the accident, Aaron's life had changed completely.

There were no more cold nights on windblown hillsides. No more endless days spent staring at the same hills and valleys, the same sheep and goats. Aaron hated getting wet when it rained and burnt when the sun was hot. At night in winter you froze, and there was always the danger of wild animals. Most of the time a shepherd's life was hard and lonely. Even people who liked it said so.

In Aaron's family there were normally two people to a watch. But soon Father would be off to Capernaum with the fleeces. They would be one short then, and John would be in charge. Aaron didn't know which was worse—to be alone on a watch, or to share it with John.

I know he will give me all the worst jobs, Aaron thought. *But I can't go back to work unless my ankle is better.* And so, whenever he felt the slightest twinge of pain, he made sure everybody knew about it.

Aaron spent most of each day sitting in the sun outside the house. There was always somebody to talk to. His grandmother sat with him and passers-by stopped to ask how he was feeling. There was Mary to boss, and his small cousins down the street to tease. And when he tired of that, he would ask somebody to help him to the village well, or to visit Great Uncle Aaron. Aaron liked his company best of all.

Great Uncle Aaron was very old. He was the best storyteller in the village. On warm days he and the other old men sat under the fig tree near the Rabbi's house. They took turns telling marvellous stories about olden times. About Abraham and Isaac. About the land before there were any towns and villages, when the people were nomads and lived in tents. Great Uncle Aaron also told stores about his own childhood. He had been born in the village and knew the history of every family. When Aaron heard that the gray-bearded old men had once been wild boys, he could hardly believe it. He laughed when he heard about the times they had hidden the women's wash, and replaced the eggs in the hen's nest with stones.

"Why, we have done that," he cried.

"You have?" teased Great Uncle Aaron.

The other old men enjoyed the stories as much as the children. They winked at each other and chuckled into their beards, and urged him to tell another one. Aaron sat with the village children who were too young to work and listened for hours.

The day before Father was to leave for Capernaum, Aaron was still complaining about the pain in his leg. John was watching the sheep. The rest of the family had gathered for the evening meal. When Rachel brushed against his leg while passing the bread, Aaron groaned.

Father dipped a hunk of bread into the bowl of vegetable stew and stared at him. "Does your leg *still* hurt?" he asked.

Aaron nodded.

It's not a lie, he thought. *It's not painful, but it throbs, which is almost the same thing.*

"Can't you walk on it at all?" Father asked.

Grandmother saved him from answering.

"There is something wrong with it, Joseph," she said. "It should be better by now."

"Indeed it should," Mother sighed.

Father reached for more stew.

"I have been thinking, Aaron," he said slowly. "It is best if you go with me tomorrow. You will be of little help to the others if you stay here and . . ."

"To Capernaum?" Aaron gasped. "Me? Go to Capernaum?"

None of the children had ever been there. Not even John. Aaron had thought he would have to wait until he was grown before he saw the town by the Sea of Galilee.

Mark and Rachel were as surprised as Aaron. The flickering lamplight caught their faces, frozen in amazement. The lamp also caught Father's face. Aaron saw him give his beard an angry tug. Too late he caught his mother's warning glance.

"What is this?" Father thundered. "Is a man not allowed to finish speaking in his own house?"

"I—I'm sorry," Aaron bent over his supper.

Please don't change your mind! he pleaded

silently.

"I was about to tell you that your mother and I think a physician should look at your ankle," Father went on in a quieter tone of voice. "He can tell us if it is broken, and how to treat it."

Grandmother shook her head.

"A physician costs money," she muttered as she softened a crust in the stew.

"The winter fleeces will bring a good price, Mother." Father scooped up a handful of olives and tossed one into his mouth. "Once they are sold I will have money enough, God willing. It is decided. Aaron will go with me to Capernaum."

Aaron saw the look of envy on Mark's face. It was gone in an instant. Rachel didn't try to hide her feelings. She was glaring at Aaron. He could easily read the unspoken question in her dark eyes. *Why should you go to Capernaum and leave us to do your share of the work?*

Aaron was glad John wasn't there. John would have said something and Father would have listened to him. Father always listened to John.

"How am I to travel that distance?" Aaron asked. He licked the gravy from his trembling fingers as he waited for an answer. What if his father hadn't thought of it?

"You will ride on top of the fleeces," Father said. "I will lead the donkey."

Aaron sat back. He tried not to let his excitement show. Rachel was watching him over the rim of her cup. He knew everything he said and did would go straight back to John.

Chapter Four

The family was up before dawn.

The fleeces were tied to the donkey's back. The pile was so high, Aaron had to be lifted on. The load swayed and Mother clapped her hands to her face.

"Be careful!" she cried. "Watch him, Joseph. Don't let him fall off, or he will have two useless legs."

"I can't walk backwards all the way to Capernaum," Father said. He sounded annoyed. "The boy will have to hold on as best he can."

"I won't fall," Aaron said. "I'm ready, Father."

"We will leave as soon as I have said goodbye to your grandmother."

Aaron watched his father duck in through the low doorway. "Hurry!" he urged under his breath. He wanted to be away before John came home. Mark had already gone to take over the day watch. Rachel was milking the goats so he didn't have to see her reproachful face.

"Aaron! Aaron!"

Mary was tugging at the hem of his robe.

"What is it?"

"I can't see you way up there. You look like a bird in a giant nest."

He grinned down at her.

"Even the Roman Emperor couldn't have a bed more comfortable than this one," he laughed.

Mary climbed up onto the bench outside the door so she could see him better.

"Will there be Romans in Capernaum?" she asked.

"Roman soldiers," Mother told her.

"They eat little girls like you, Mary." Aaron rolled his eyes and licked his lips. "They roast them and then . . . ."

Mary screamed.

"Aaron," Mother said. "Stop it."

"Aaron be silent," Father called from the house. "Not one more word until we leave."

Aaron settled back on the fleeces. He had once seen a party of Roman soldiers march through the village. The old people had covered their faces and cursed as they went by. Aaron and his brothers had watched the soldiers openmouthed. They were the biggest men they had ever seen. Their hair was the color of ripe wheat. They had gleaming breastplates and swords and helmets with bright plumes. The sound of their marching feet and clanking armor had attracted every boy in the village. The boys lined the street long after the cloud of dust had settled and the column had disappeared from sight.

That night Father had told John and Aaron and Mark about the Romans and how they had conquered the land.

"Land that belongs to God," he said. "They

have defiled it! One day God will take his revenge."

"When?" Aaron wanted to know.

"In God's good time," Father told him. "Until then, keep away from the Romans for they are dangerous."

The thought that Aaron might see Roman soldiers in Capernaum filled Aaron with a delicious mixture of fear and excitement.

Mary was sent indoors for a cloth-wrapped bundle, and a goatskin bag of water. They were given to Aaron to hold.

"There is cheese and bread in the cloth," Mother said. "And some dried fig cakes. Enough food to last the journey. When will you be home again, Joseph?"

"A day to walk there. Two days to arrange a good price for the fleeces. A day to find a physician, and home again," he answered. "Are you comfortable, Aaron? We must go, or we will never be there by nightfall."

Father gathered Mary in a hug that made her squeal.

"May God watch over you all until our return," he said as he kissed his wife.

There was no escaping John after all. He was waiting for them at the side of the road outside the village. He wanted to go over the work to be done while they were away. For a brief moment his eyes rested on Aaron's bad ankle. Aaron's heart lurched, but John didn't say a word about it. He talked to Father about the flock as if Aaron wasn't there.

Aaron was glad. He lay back on the fleeces with a sigh of relief. He closed his eyes as their voices droned on. He didn't open them again until he heard John say "Go with God, Father" and the donkey started to move.

"And you, my son."

"You too, Aaron," John called.

Aaron avoided John's eyes as he raised his hand in a farewell salute. He felt a twinge of guilt. There would be a lot of extra work with the two of them away.

I can't walk, so I wouldn't be much help if I stayed, he told himself. *Father said so himself. There is no point in feeling guilty.*

The journey to Capernaum was an exciting experience for Aaron. He had never been closer than an hour's walk from the village before. From his high perch he could see everything. The line of distant hills that changed shape and color the closer they came to them. The forests and the flower-scattered hillsides. The villages tucked into folds in the hills. The fields of bright green vegetables that filled the valleys. In the distance he could see flocks of sheep. He didn't envy the lonely shepherds watching him.

It was a long while since Aaron had had his father to himself. He was sure nobody else had a father who was such good company. When Aaron wanted to be quiet and watch the ribbon of road unfold before them, Father was quiet too. When Aaron grew bored and said "Tell me a story," he always had a story ready to tell. His great laugh echoed back through the rocky passes. He called a pleasant greeting to everybody they met.

They passed other travelers along the way. There were men traveling in groups or striding alone, their long robes flapping around their sandaled feet. Some men rode by on donkeys. The sure-footed animals picked their way over rocks and potholes. Once Aaron and his father had to make way for a rumbling cart piled high with a family's belongings. On top of a pile of bedding sat a woman with a baby in her arms. Children walked in the dust behind the cart. Aaron wished there was time to ask where the family came from and where they were going.

Because the donkey was heavily laden, the journey took Aaron and his father longer than expected. Darkness fell before Capernaum came into sight. They came to a village. Father left Aaron by the well while he went to find a man he knew. Holding a lamp high to light the way, the man led them to a cave that served as a stable.

"You are welcome to a night's shelter here," he said.

Father carried Aaron to a straw-filled corner. It felt good to be out of the cold night wind. The warm air smelled of animals, and made Aaron feel sleepy. He could hardly stay awake long enough to eat some supper.

"Here, drink some of this fresh goats milk," Father urged.

Eyes closing, Aaron drained the cup and fell back on the straw. He was asleep before his father had time to cover him.

Aaron would never forget his first sight of Capernaum and the Sea of Galilee, Early the next morning they came to the top of a hill. The town lay below them, the pale blue of the Sea of Galilee reflecting the morning sky. The sea was so big the hills on the far side were a dark purple color. Fishing boats were skimming over the surface, their sails looking like clusters of cream colored butterflies. They looked so tiny from the hilltop that Aaron thought he could hold them in the palm of his hand.

The town was a jumble of buildings. There were more houses than he could count. Small sand colored buildings nestled against big ones. He could see narrow, winding streets and open squares shaded by trees.

And there were people. Looking like ants from this distance, there were more people than Aaron had ever seen in his life.

"What do you think of it all?" Father asked.

When Aaron didn't answer, Father's laugh filled the morning air.

"I have never seen you speechless before, my son."

"It . . . . it's wonderful," Aaron gasped.

Chapter Five

There were plenty of other people heading towards the town. At a crossroads they passed a cart pulled by two oxen. The back was full of vegetables. Even Aaron's heavily-laden donkey could move faster than the lumbering oxen.

Next, they caught up with a boy shepherding some sheep down the hill. The boy was whistling as he used his staff to keep the sheep together.

As Aaron and his father passed the sheep, they heard hooves pounding along behind them. A Roman soldier galloped by. His horse was covered with sweat, his breastplate coated with dust. The sheep scattered in fright. The donkey stopped dead. Aaron wasn't holding on. He pitched forward over the donkey's head.

"Father!" he cried as he slid towards the ground.

Father caught him just in time. Aaron heard him mutter something under his breath as he stared after the soldier.

"You were told to hold on!" He sounded angry.

"Have you forgotten your mother's warning?"

He helped Aaron back onto the fleeces. When they were underway again, Aaron held on tight to the ropes that bound them. There was so much to see, he didn't know where to look.

They made their way through the center of town. The narrow streets were lined with open-fronted shops. Aaron thought of the small carpenter's shop at home where his friend Peter worked. Here, there were so many carpenter's shops he didn't have time to count them all.

The streets were crowded and noisy. Aaron listened to the babble of voices, the clang of metal against metal, the steady rat-a-tat-tat of hammers. Chickens squawked as they were carried to market, tied by their legs in great feathery bunches. Donkeys brayed. Street sellers shouted their wares. One street in Capernaum was busier than Aaron's whole village on market day.

Two boys on the flat roof of a house pointed at Aaron as he rode by. They were laughing.

"Are you comfortable on your throne, your majesty?" one yelled.

"Get down and walk you lazy good-for-nothing," jeered the other.

Aaron turned his head so they couldn't see his red face. He was glad when his father led the donkey around a corner, and they were out of sight.

"Put me down somewhere, Father," he begged.

They had reached the waterfront. Father lifted him down.

"Wait here," he said. "I won't be long. I will leave the fleeces at my cousin Mark's warehouse and come back for you."

As Father walked away, Aaron could still feel the swaying movement of the donkey. He steadied himself with his staff. His ankle throbbed even when he lifted it off the ground. He sat down on a rock at the edge of the beach. When he rested his bad leg on another rock, the throbbing stopped.

There was plenty to look at while he was waiting. Fishing boats were pulled up on the sand. Nets were strung up to dry. An old man with a bushy gray beard was mending a hole in a net.

It was midmorning, and the sun was hot. The water looked cool and inviting.

I wonder if I could hop to the water's edge? Aaron thought. *It's not far.*

He managed to make it with the help of his staff, and sat down in ankle deep water. It felt deliciously cool against his hot skin.

He wriggled further out. He ducked his head underwater and drank his fill. The water washed the dust of the journey from his body. The waves gently lifted his bad leg and lapped around his ankle. It throbbed, but not as badly as before.

"That's better," he sighed.

After a few minutes in the water, the throbbing stopped altogether. Had the water cured it?

Aaron tried to stand. The throbbing started up again. He collapsed back into the water with a groan of disappointment.

Aaron had never learned to swim. He stayed in shallow water. He put his staff under his knees and used his hands on the bottom to work his way along to the nearest fishing boat. The anchor rope disappeared out into deeper water. Aaron caught hold of the rope and hauled himself up onto the beach. He hopped back on the rock, cool and refreshed.

Aaron watched a fishing boat pull in. Its net was full of silvery fish. The fishermen tossed the fish into baskets and carried them to some nearby market stalls. Aaron struggled to his feet and hopped along behind them. There was a flight of steps near the stalls. He crawled up the steps on his hands and knees. From the top he could see everything. The noisy bustle of the fish market was just below him. Beyond the stalls were the boats, and beyond the boats was the vast stretch of water.

Aaron was still sitting at the top of the steps when his father came back.

"Oh Father, I love it here," he said. "Everything a person could want is right here in Capernaum."

Father sat down beside him and frowned.

"Everything? Where is the sweet air of Galilee?" he demanded. "Not here, for sure. This place stinks of fish and worse."

Aaron hadn't noticed the strong smell of fish.

"But look at the people, Father. I have never seen so many in my life."

"There are too many," Father grumbled.

Aaron tugged at his sleeve. "Look down there," he whispered.

A Roman lady was being carried by. She lay on a bed among a pile of brightly colored pillows. The bed had handles at each end. Two black slaves, their muscles bulging, were carrying the bed. Another slave walked alongside. He shaded the lady from the midday sun with a leaf-shaped fan. The small party stopped at the foot of the steps.

"She must be rich," Aaron gasped. "Look at her gold jewelry, Father. And her skin. It is as white as her dress. I wish Rachel and Mary could see her."

"I am glad they cannot," Father said fiercely. "Her skin is white because she is idle. She is nothing more than a perfumed ornament. Has she not legs under her gown? Why doesn't she walk like everybody else?"

"Maybe she hurt herself like me," Aaron said.

"How can such a woman hurt herself?" Father scoffed. "I am sure she never puts a foot to the ground without a slave to help her."

A girl in a plain blue gown carried a basket of fish over to the bed. As the Roman lady examined them, she held an orange studded with cloves to her nose.

"See, Father? There is somebody else who doesn't like the smell of fish," Aaron teased.

Father laughed, but then his face darkened.

He indicated the Roman lady and her slaves with a scornful wave. "That is why I like the simple life of a shepherd, Aaron. There are no scenes like that to keep my thoughts from God. I am a plain man, used to plain ways. Everytime I come to Capernaum I long for the peace and quiet of my beloved hills. Oh, how I long to be home."

Aaron didn't long to be home. He hadn't thought about the hills once since they had left them.

They were to stay with Father's cousin Mark. Cousin Mark lived alone in a small house at the edge of town. His wife had died and he had no children. His work was the buying and selling of fleeces. He had promised Aaron's father a good price.

"Depending on the quality," he said when Aaron and Father arrived at his house. "I haven't seen them yet."

"Our fleeces are of the finest," Aaron blurted out. "You will not find better ones anywhere."

"Aaron, be silent," Father said with a quick frown.

"Let the boy talk, Joseph," Cousin Mark said. "On what do you base your knowledge, Aaron?"

"We have worked to improve the quality this past year." Aaron stopped and flushed. "I mean, Father and John have. The fleeces are thick and the wool is pure. You will find no thorns or burrs in our wool."

Cousin Mark smiled.

"You will make a good shepherd, Aaron."

"A shepherd? Not me," Aaron said. He darted a look at his father. "I don't like the life. It is too . . too lonely. And I hate sheep. They are so stupid . . ."

Father shook his head in mock disgust.

"Listen to the boy. Did you ever meet a shepherd who hates his sheep? What am I to do with him?" He leaned over and rumpled Aaron's curly hair. Aaron sighed inwardly.

It's always the same, he thought. *Every time I try to tell Father how I feel, he thinks I am joking. Why won't he take me seriously?*

Cousin Mark wasn't laughing. He was looking at Aaron with interest.

"If you hate your father's sheep, how is it you have studied the quality of their fleeces?" he wanted to know.

"I overheard Father and John discussing them,"

Aaron said honestly. "I like to listen to people talking. Especially if they know what they are talking about. If Father says they are the best we have ever produced, then it is true."

Father laughed. "Thank you, my son," he said. He turned to his cousin. "The truth is that Aaron sat on the fleeces all the way here, so he is speaking from personal experience as to their softness and lack of thorns. Am I right, Aaron?"

Aaron laughed and nodded. "Could I go with you when you put them up for sale?" he asked eagerly.

It looked as if Cousin Mark was about to agree, but Father spoke first.

"No, Aaron. It would be different if you could walk. We can't carry you around the market. Business is business."

"It will take a while to find the right buyer and settle on a fair price," Cousin Mark explained. "These things cannot be rushed. Can you entertain yourself for a day or two?"

Aaron nodded. He wanted to say "Take as long as you wish" but he knew his father would be angry. Several times on the way to Capernaum Father had said he was worried about how John and Mark would manage while they were away.

Aaron made the most of every minute of his stay in Capernaum. Each morning Father helped him onto the donkey. He took him down to the water and left him there while he went with Cousin Mark to haggle over prices. If Aaron wanted to leave the beach, he had to manage by himself.

He wanted to see everything, the shops and the markets, the Roman garrison outside the town and the synagogue. At first he hopped. Then, when his ankle started to feel better, he hobbled, leaning on his staff. The more he used his leg, the less it hurt.

On the third day, he met Benjamin.

The two boys sat on the wall for a long time after the cured man had carried his bed away. Aaron wanted to see the man who could work miracles. They waited through the hottest part of the day. From time to time the door of the house opened, but Jesus didn't come out.

"I'm thirsty," Benjamin said around midafternoon. "Let's go down to the water and I will show you our fishing boat. Sometimes Jesus walks along the beach and talks to people. Maybe we will see him there later."

Aaron spent the rest of the day with Benjamin. His new friend knew a lot about boats and fishing. Aaron decided the life of a fisherman was a lot more exciting than watching sheep.

Jesus didn't come to the beach, but Aaron's father did. He came at dusk to tell Aaron it was time for the evening meal. As the two boys said goodbye, Benjamin said, "I'm going fishing early in the morning. My father says you can go too, if you like."

"Yes please!" Aaron cried. He could hardly wait.

Over supper, Aaron talked of nothing but the paralyzed man.

"Have you heard about Jesus of Nazareth, Cousin Mark?" he asked. "Have you seen him?"

"Yes, I have. People come from far and near to be cured by him. His fame will soon spread as far as your village, you wait and see." He looked at Aaron and chuckled. "It is lucky your leg is getting better by itself. It saves us the trouble of asking Jesus to heal you."

Aaron grinned and studied his ankle.

"It is better," he agreed. "Each day it hurts less."

"I know," Father said. "I have been watching you. When I came down to the beach tonight, you were so eager to tell me about your day, you almost ran towards me. God is good. There will be no need for a physician for you, my son."

Aaron was glad. He didn't want a stranger poking his ankle and giving him medicine to drink. He grinned at his father. The grin froze when he heard Father's next words.

"Because you are so much better, I am going to send you home, Aaron. It is not fair for you to stay here and enjoy yourself while your brothers and Rachel do all the work."

Chapter Six

The news was so unexpected, Aaron's heart dropped like a stone.

"Send me home?" he echoed. "Have you sold the fleeces?"

"Not yet. I am sending you home alone."

"Alone?" Aaron gasped. "How? When?"

"Tomorrow at dawn."

"Tomorrow? But I promised Benjamin . . . . ."

"Promised him what? To spend the day in idle play?" Father was tugging at his beard.

"We were going fishing. I was going to help on his father's fishing boat," Aaron said wildly.

"You would help a stranger, but not your own family?" Father shook his head in disbelief. "You expect them to shoulder your share of the work forever? The reason for you to be here has gone, Aaron. You must go home."

"But my ankle . . ."

"It is better."

"It still hurts."

"You can walk on it. If you can walk around town, you can walk after the sheep."

"But I . . ."

"Enough!" Father thundered. Aaron had never seen him look so angry. "You cannot walk that far, so I have arranged for you to ride in a cart. It will be passing through our village. The driver has promised to see you safely home. To bed with you, Aaron. I will wake you in the morning."

Aaron could not sleep. The thought of leaving Capernaum so soon was more than he could bear. As he stared into the velvety darkness, his brain searched desperately for some way to stay.

I could run away and hide somewhere, he thought.

It might work, for a while. Sooner or later Father would find him. What was the point in staying in Capernaum only to skulk around like a thief afraid of capture?

If I ran away, I couldn't stay in town, he decided. *Cousin Mark knows too many people. I would never be able to show my face. I might have to leave Galilee altogether.*

That was too big a step to take. Aaron knew Father would never forgive him. To be forever cut off from his family wasn't what Aaron wanted at all.

A few more days, he thought. *If only I could stay until Father goes home! If I could manage to miss the cart he would have to let me stay. But how can I do it without anyone suspecting anything?*

A sleepless hour passed while Aaron went over the possibilities. There was only one that might work. Maybe he could convince his father that his ankle had become worse overnight.

If Father believed him, which was doubtful, a

physician would be called. The physician would see through the trick and then there would be trouble.

Father will lock me up rather than let me enjoy myself until it was time for us to leave, Aaron thought. *I would be in the biggest trouble of my life.*

There was nothing else Aaron could think of, and he fell into an unhappy sleep.

Father woke him in the dead light just before dawn. When Aaron got up he limped and complained of pain. Not much, just enough to see what would happen.

Father tugged at his beard and said, "Don't make me angry, Aaron."

They dressed in silence.

"Is there time for me to go and say goodbye to Benjamin?" Aaron asked when he was ready.

Father shook his head.

"But I told him I would go fishing this morning. They will be waiting for me."

"I have sent a message to the boat," Father said. He put his arm around Aaron's shoulders. "Don't look so upset, my son. Think how lucky you are to have been here. You have enjoyed yourself, haven't you?"

"Yes," Aaron sighed.

"Then be thankful. Your memories will go home with you. No one can ever take them away from you. They will be like treasures that you can take out of storage whenever you please. Think of the stories you will be able to tell when you get home."

His words didn't make Aaron feel any happier. Aaron said goodbye to Cousin Mark in a daze of disappointment.

Aaron was to ride home in a cart delivering clay jars used for the storage of oil, wine and grain. When Aaron and Father arrived at the pottery shop outside the town, the big empty jars were being loaded on the straw-lined cart.

"It won't be such a comfortable ride this time," Father joked.

Aaron was silent. He was afraid if he tried to speak, he would cry instead.

The driver said he was ready to go. Aaron climbed into the cart and squeezed into a corner. He sat down and stared dully at the fingerprints in the rough clay of the nearest jar. He hardly heard the stream of messages his father was giving him.

The cart was pulled by two oxen. As they started their slow way out of the potter's field, Father walked alongside.

"Don't forget to tell your mother I will be home before the Sabbath," he said. "Tell John I will buy another donkey if I can afford it. Go with God, my son."

Aaron felt Father's rough hand on the back of his neck. The big hand was so gentle, Aaron could hold back the tears no longer. As they trickled down his cheeks, he did not dare look up. He couldn't bear Father to see that he was crying.

The hand lifted, and was gone. Aaron rubbed his wet face on his sleeve. When he finally peeped over the side of the cart, Father was mounting the donkey. Weak with misery, Aaron slumped back in his corner.

The oxen strained to pull the heavy load up the

hill. They were at the top before Aaron looked back again.

Capernaum lay below them, half hidden by swirls of early morning mist. He could see fishing boats out on the water.

Benjamin must be on one of those boats, he thought. *Did he receive the message before they sailed? Or is he wondering where I am?*

Beyond the town Aaron could see the outline of the Roman garrison. Benjamin's father supplied the camp with fish. Benjamin had offered to take Aaron there to see the soldiers parade for a visiting general. "I know a guard who will let us in the gate," he had said.

Aaron thought about the plans he and Benjamin had made. There were so many things to do in a town as big as Capernaum. Most of all, Aaron had wanted to see the teacher from Nazareth. He had seen Benjamin's aunt when she came down to the fishing boat. Benjamin had pointed her out. She looked like everybody else. Aaron would never have guessed she had had a skin disease so horrible nobody wanted to go near her.

"What kind of man can work a miracle just by touching someone?" he had wondered out loud.

Benjamin had told him sometimes he didn't even do that. "Begone!" he had said to a man with a devil inside him, and the devil had left the man's body. Some men Benjamin knew had seen it happen.

Jesus was a mystery Aaron had hoped to solve. Now it was too late.

Aaron was glad the driver of the cart showed no sign of wanting to talk. He was too lost in his own misery to want to make conversation with a stranger. He sat in numb silence the whole of that long day. How different this journey was from the one with Father!

From time to time they stopped in a village to unload some of the jars. As soon as there was room, Aaron stretched out his legs. He had some food in a cloth, and a goatskin of water. He wasn't hungry, but he ate to pass the time. The cart moved so slowly he was sure he could have walked faster, even with his bad leg.

You don't want to get there any quicker, he reminded himself. *As soon as John sees you he will want you to go back to work.* Back to the lonely, boring hillsides.

The road grew worse as the day wore on. The cart lurched over holes and rocks. Aaron wished he had thought to ask Father for a fleece to put under his leg. Bounced against the planking, it was starting to ache.

The sun went down and they still hadn't reached the village. There were four jars left. The driver had tied them down with rope.

It had been a long uncomfortable, unhappy day and Aaron was weary. He gathered the straw into a pile and made himself a bed. As the cart rumbled along, he fell into a light sleep.

A pain in his left leg woke him up. By the light of the moon he could see the jars had broken loose, rolling against his ankle. He pushed it away with his staff. The cart lurched and another jar rolled against him. The road was so uneven, as fast as he pushed the jars away they rolled back again. They were big and heavy and they hurt.

"Stop!"

At Aaron's shout, the driver hauled on the reins.

"The jars keep hitting my leg," Aaron told him. When he touched his ankle it felt sore.

"It isn't far now," the driver said as he retied the jars. "You will soon be home."

Aaron lay back. The next thing he knew, somebody was shining a light in his face.

"He's asleep," a familiar voice said. It was his mother. "He looks so pale. Is he ill?"

"He was complaining about his leg," the driver said.

"Where is my husband?"

"He said he had to stay longer in Capernaum."

"Is my son's leg the reason he sent him home?"

"I don't know. The boy hardly spoke a word to me. I thought it strange. A boy his age is usually full of life."

"Did my husband say anything?"

"Only that I was to deliver him to you."

Aaron stirred and opened his eyes. The light moved away. His mother put a gentle hand on his forehead and smoothed back his hair.

"Lie still," she murmured. "We will carry you to bed. Go back to sleep. We will talk in he morning."

Aaron felt himself being lifted up. When his leg knocked against the doorpost, he groaned.

"The poor lamb!" Grandmother was somewhere close by.

"Lay him down on his pallet."

Other voices spoke, only to be shushed. Someone covered him. The cart rumbled away. The light went out. Through the darkness Aaron overheard a whispered conversation.

"Why did Joseph send him home?" Mother sounded worried.

"It must be because of his ankle," Grandmother answered. "How does he look?"

"Worse than when he left us! He looks so pale. Oh Mother, he looks terrible."

"I thought so. I knew there was something wrong. I could tell by the way he gasped that he was in pain."

"But Joseph said he was going to consult a physician."

"Maybe the physician said there is nothing to be done."

"Don't say such a thing!" Mother gasped.

"It must be so. He was carried to Capernaum and carried home in a worse state. What does that tell you?"

There was a long silence.

"We can do nothing except pray and then sleep," Grandmother whispered. "Aaron will tell us all about it in the morning."

Chapter Seven

It was a while before Aaron slept. The whispered conversation had given him an idea.

If Mother and Grandmother thought his leg was still bad, he wouldn't have to go back to work. John and the others had managed so far. Surely they could manage for another day or so.

No one can be expected to go from Capernaum straight back to watching the flock, Aaron reasoned. *It will take me a while to adjust to the change.*

The dangerous part of letting Mother think his leg was no better was that she would find out the truth when Father came home. *Unless . . . . .* Aaron frowned into the darkness . . . . . *unless she thinks it was getting better until the jars rolled into it. I could let her think that. Those jars are heavy.* He remembered how John had once dropped an empty grain jar on his toe. It had been painful for days.

Aaron's fingers groped under the quilt. The skin around his left ankle felt tight yet soft like a ripe grape. It was a lot fatter than the other one.

It hurt when he squeezed it.

Maybe by morning it will hurt more, he thought hopefully, and fell asleep.

Aaron awoke at dawn. Cozy and warm under his quilt, he listened to the household stirring.

He heard John get up and leave for the hillsides. Mark wasn't there, so he must have had the night watch. If John had gone to relieve him, it meant he wouldn't be home until nightfall.

All the better! Aaron thought.

Soon after Rachel left to milk the goats, Mark came home. He asked about Aaron but Mother shushed him. Aaron pretended to be asleep when Mark unrolled his pallet and laid down beside him.

Rachel came home with the milk and left again. She took some food with her. That meant she wouldn't be home until nightfall either.

When Grandmother got up, Aaron could hear her complaining about her back. Through half-closed eyes he watched her hobble outside.

"Help me carry the quilts up to the roof, Mary," he heard Mother say. "Then I want you to run some errands."

When they had gone there was no one indoors except Aaron and Mark.

Aaron flexed his leg under the quilt. It ached, but there was no sharp pain. He sat up and looked over at Mark. His brother was sound asleep.

With an eye on the door, Aaron stood up. In the half-light he could see his ankle was swollen. He put his weight on it and took a few steps. It throbbed, but not as much as he had hoped.

Outside, his mother called to someone. With a

glance at Mark, Aaron sat down on the edge of the sleeping platform. He eased himself down onto the dirt floor. Using his arms and his good leg, he crawled over to the doorway.

Grandmother was sitting on the bench. Mother was talking to a neighbor.

"Aaron?" she called. "Where are you going?"

"Nowhere," he called back. He sat down in the dust and stretched out his legs. His ankle was bruised as well as swollen. In the bright sunlight it looked much worse than it felt. Aaron hid a smile of triumph as she hurried towards him.

"Your ankle is far worse," she said as she bent over him. "Where did those bruises come from?"

"On the way home the jars broke loose and . . . and one of them fell on my leg," Aaron answered quickly. He knew the jars hadn't fallen, but rolled against his ankles. Whe she didn't say anything he added, "They were big jars, the ones for storing oil and grain. You know how heavy they are. I hope it isn't broken this time."

"Does it hurt more than the first time?" Grandmother asked.

"Oh, Mother, if only you could see it," Aaron's mother said before he could think of an answer. "It is swollen again and I have never seen such bruises. It must be agony."

Grandmother leaned down and ran her cool dry fingers over both ankles. Her touch was as gentle as a breeze, but Aaron groaned.

"I can feel the difference," she said. "What did the physician say about it?"

"I didn't see one because . . . because it seemed to be getting better," Aaron explained. He started to sweat. He had almost made the mistake of saying "because we couldn't find one." Mother would be bound to ask Father why he couldn't find a physician in a town the size of Capernaum.

"When is your father coming home?" Mother asked.

"He said I was to tell you he would be home before the Sabbath."

Aaron waited for her to ask more questions. How much better was your ankle? Could you walk at all? What did your father say about it? Why didn't he keep you with him until he had sold the fleeces?

She didn't ask any of them. The ankle, now dark with bruises was all the evidence she needed.

"You are not to try and stand on that leg until the swelling has gone down," was all she said. Grandmother didn't ask him any more questions either.

"Mary?" she cried. "Where is Mary?"

"I'm here, Grandmother."

"Bring me cool water and a cloth. Hurry. I am going to bathe Aaron's ankle."

Aaron relaxed as the womenfolk fussed around him. It had all been so easy he wanted to laugh out loud.

He spent the morning entertaining Mary and his grandmother with tales of the things he had seen in Capernaum. His small cousins came to see him as soon as they heard he was home. Other children followed them. Soon Aaron had a circle of eager listeners. When the sun grew too hot he crawled over to a shady grapevine. His audience moved with him. Aaron felt like his great uncle as the children listened to his stories openmouthed.

He told them about the boats and the market, the synagogue and the shops, the Romans he had seen and Father's cousin Mark. He talked about Benjamin too, but he didn't mention the miracle of the paralyzed man. It was there all the time, in the back of his mind, but he didn't want to talk about it. There were too many unanswered questions.

I wish I had seen Jesus of Nazareth, he thought. *I wish I had heard him preach.* Most of all Aaron wished he had seen a miracle.

Every hour Grandmother bathed his ankle and wrapped it in a damp cloth. The bruises looked much worse when they were wet. The children gasped when they saw them and Grandmother shook her head and murmured, "The poor lamb." Aaron felt guilty, but only for a moment. There were more stories to tell and a circle of eager listeners.

At midday, Mary brought him some food and a cool drink to ease his tired throat. Aaron leaned back in the shade and sighed with pleasure.

If I could stay in the village all the time, I wouldn't mind being home so much, he thought.

He was in the middle of telling the children about Benjamin when Mark joined them. He came out of the house, stretching and yawning.

"Benjamin showed me all over his father's fishing boat," Aaron was saying.

"What was it like?" a small boy asked. "I have never seen a fishing boat."

"It has sails and . . . . . ."

"How did you manage to climb all over a boat when you can't walk?" Mark asked.

Aaron looked at him warily. If John had asked the question it would have been because he was suspicious. Mark wasn't that kind of person, but it was better to be careful.

"On a boat there are plenty of things to hold on to," he said.

"How did you get *to* the boat?" Mark asked. He had big dark circles under his eyes and he sounded tired.

"Father left me down by the water each morning. I could hop." Aaron paused and thought carefully before he spoke. "Benjamin helped me. I—I could walk a little with help. But then on the way home a jar fell on my ankle."

Mark grunted. "They are not *that* heavy," he said.

"It was one of the big grain jars," Aaron said quickly. "It was dark and I was asleep. The driver . . . the driver had to lift it off."

Mark was always so quick to be kind and thoughtful. "Poor Father," he said.

"Why poor Father?" Mary said.

"Because he will blame himself for sending Aaron home alone. He will feel terrible when he finds out what happened. You know how kind-hearted he is."

It was true about Father's kind heart. He and Mark were a lot alike. Aaron felt himself go hot all over. He had never thought that Father might feel guilty.

"Why did Father send you home alone, Aaron?"

The question took Aaron by surprise. He had expected it from John or Rachel, but not from Mark. To cover his confusion he leaned forward and rearranged the cloth around his ankle.

"Aaron?" Mark was staring at him as if Aaron was a person he didn't like very much.

He's changed while I have been away, Aaron thought. *It's almost as if he is older than me, not the other way around.*

"I *told* you. It was starting to get better. Just a little. I still couldn't walk by myself but . . . ."

"Then why didn't you stay in Capernaum with Father? Were you misbehaving? Is that why he sent you home early?"

Aaron avoided the question by taking a long drink of water. Better Mark should think he had been involved in some childish prank, than find out the truth. Mark took his silence for guilt.

"So that's what it was," he said. "I would give anything to see Capernaum. I would work until I dropped if Father would take me with him. But no, he took you, and you repay him by misbehaving. It's not fair, Aaron. I have been working like a beast of burden, and you . . . ."

"Stop it, Mark!" Grandmother's voice was sharp with anger. "What does it matter *why* Aaron came home? He is injured and he cannot walk. He needs your kindness, not your jealousy."

Mark turned and ran off down the street. Aaron watched him until he was out of sight.

If Mark is this angry, what will John say? he wondered with a sinking heart.

Chapter Eight

John had a lot to say about Aaron's mysterious accident in the cart. He questioned him closely. Aaron was saved by Mother and Grandmother. Mother said John was being unfair. Grandmother said he was upsetting Aaron. Mother forbade him to question Aaron at all.

Once again Aaron made the most of his injury. The swelling went down and the bruises started to fade, so he had to make a bigger fuss about the pain. When Mother tried to make him stand and exercise his leg, he said he couldn't do it.

Aaron was enjoying his escape from work much more this time. He had stories of his own to tell. Everyone in the village wanted to hear about Capernaum. Everyone except John and Mark and Rachel.

The day before the Sabbath, Rachel went to the village well for water. While she was waiting her turn, she heard a stranger asking for her family. The traveler, on his way from Capernaum to Cana, had a message from Father. He would not be home for a few more days. Cousin

Mark was sick. Because he lived alone, Father didn't want to leave him. He would hurry home as soon as Mark was better.

Aaron was the only person in the family who was happy that Father was not coming home.

I'll start walking again in a day or so, he decided. *There is no rush now that Father will be away longer.*

Everything was going Aaron's way. He had been helping with some of the women's chores, but there wasn't much he could do. It meant he had a lot of free time. The first day he crawled wherever he wanted to go. He had even crawled as far as Great Uncle Aaron's house. People had stared at him as he made his slow way along the dusty streets. It had made him feel like a beggar, but there was nothing else he could do. It was his friend Peter who had solved the problem.

Peter was the son of the village carpenter. They had been friends for as long as Aaron could remember. He was a grown man of eighteen, but he wasn't much taller than Aaron. There had been something wrong with his legs from birth. They had never grown to match the rest of his body. He had the chest and arms of a man, but his legs were like two useless sticks. Peter had never been able to walk. He got around the village on a small cart with a handle for pulling.

Because Peter lived behind the shop, he didn't need the cart very often. When he offered to lend it to Aaron, Aaron was overjoyed.

"You may use it on one condition," Peter said.

"What condition?"

"That you visit the shop and tell us about Capernaum."

"I'll come every day," Aaron promised.

Before his trip, Aaron had wanted to become a carpenter. The bustle of the carpenter's shop had always attracted him. He liked to watch Peter and his father at work. It fascinated him to see them turn a shapeless piece of wood into something useful. He liked the smell of the wood shavings. He loved to watch the color of the wood change when it was rubbed with oil. The shop was a busy place. There was always somebody stopping in to place an order or pick one up. There was always time for a story to be told, or news to be exchanged. A carpenter's life was never lonely.

Aaron sat in Peter's cart, and Mary pulled it along. She was little, but she was strong. Aaron pretended to be a Roman officer in a chariot.

"Go faster, slave!" he yelled until Mary threatened to tip him out. They had a lot of fun when Mary pulled him through the village in Peter's cart.

The first time Mother saw the cart, she said, "The girls could pull you up into the hills to help watch the sheep."

"The cart is too low," Aaron said. "It will only work where the ground is flat and there are no rocks." He was glad what he said was true. It made him feel less guilty when his brothers came home white-faced with weariness.

Each morning Aaron decided to put off walking one more day. There was no rush now that he had the cart. At home, everything was within easy reach. He hardly stood up at all.

As long as I am back to work when Father comes home, he told himself. *Mother and Grand-*

mother are on my side. If John complains again, they will stick up for me.

Early one morning, Aaron was asleep on his pallet when something poked him in the ribs. He opened his eyes to see John bending over him. It wasn't yet light but Aaron could tell his brother was angry.

"I thought you had the night watch," Aaron mumbled, half asleep.

"I do, but I have come home early. Mark and I decided it is time you went back to work, Aaron," John's voice was low enough so that Mother couldn't hear. "Get up."

Mark was sitting up on his pallet. He looked sleepy and upset.

"It's not fair, Aaron," he whispered. "We have been doing your share of the work long enough."

Aaron pulled his quilt up around his shoulders.

"I've told you a hundred times," he whispered back. "I have tried to walk and I can't, so how can I get back to the flock?"

"We will carry you. We will make sure you get there, don't worry about *that.*" John's voice rose. "Listen to me, Aaron. I have been on watch all night. I am cold and I am tired and I have had enough of your nonsense. Get up before I . . . ."

John was holding his staff. As he raised it, Aaron yelped and ducked under his quilt.

"John! Leave your brother alone!" Mother called out of the darkness. "It is not yet morning and already you boys are quarreling. Why are you home? Who is with the flock?"

"Cousin Matthew."

"Why? What is this all about?"

Aaron was glad Mother couldn't see the unhappy look on Mark's face.

"You said I could go to market with you today, Mother," Mark reminded her. "Please make Aaron get up and take a turn . . ."

"He can't Mark." Her voice was firm. "You will have to guard the flock again today."

"But you said . . . ."

"I said if Aaron was better you could go with me. He's not, and so he can't watch the sheep. What would happen if some of them strayed while he is keeping watch? How would he fetch them back? If we lose a lamb because he can't run after it, will you be responsible?"

There was no answer to that. Mark sighed and got up.

"Our sheep hardly ever stray," he muttered as he rolled up his quilt and pallet. "I don't see why Aaron can't keep watch this once."

He sighed again and walked over to the door. John was still glaring down at Aaron. He bent and caught hold of the edge of his quilt.

"You little . . ." he hissed.

Aaron let out a yelp of fear.

"For the last time, John. Leave Aaron alone."

"I didn't touch him," John growled. "But I would like to. When Father comes home he is going to hear all about this spoiled little play-actor."

As Aaron snuggled down under the goatskin quilt he felt a twinge in his ankle. He gasped, making sure it was loud enough for John to hear. Sometimes he hoped his ankle would never get better. Then they would be sorry. After all, he hadn't fallen down the hillside on purpose!

Chapter Nine

Aaron didn't want to be home when John got up. As soon as Mary had finished her chores, he asked her to pull him to the carpenter's shop. He stayed there all day. When he came home for the evening meal John was getting ready for the night watch. Aaron could see his temper was still simmering.

"Father will see through you," he said to Aaron as they sat down to eat.

"John, please," Mother said as she passed him a bowl of soup.

"I don't care. I have had enough of his tricks," John growled. "When Father comes home he will make Aaron work! There will be enough for us for two to a watch so that will put an end to Aaron's excuses."

Aaron pretended he hadn't heard. He watched Rachel trimming the lamps as if he had never seen her do it before.

"Are you listening, Aaron?" John challenged him. "I'm going to ask Father to put you on night watch with me. Then I am going to tie you to a tree and use you as bait for wild animals!" As he spoke he stared at Aaron and slowly ripped a hunk of bread in half.

Grandmother threw up her hands in horror. "Listen to the boy."

Rachel was laughing. "He is only teasing, Grandmother."

"Teasing? You call that teasing?" she cried.

"Don't say such things, John," Mother said.

"Why not? John demanded, his eyes flashing. "Aaron deserves it. He does nothing but enjoy himself. He rides around like a king in that cart while the rest of us do his work. I'm tired of spending night after night out in the cold because he's too lazy to work. If I had my way I would feed him to the wild animals slice by slice."

Grandmother gasped. "You wicked boy," she cried. "Are you saying that Aaron is pretending? Why would he make up the pain of a crippled leg?"

"Because it suits him, isn't that so, Aaron?" John wiped out his bowl with some bread and got to his feet.

To Aaron's relief, John didn't wait for an answer. He walked over to the door and picked up his cloak and his staff and disappeared out into the star-filled night.

"I'm not crippled, Grandmother," Aaron said when he had gone. The word made him shiver.

Grandmother dipped her bread in her soup and sighed.

"I'm not! I'm not like Peter. My leg will get better. It is taking longer than expected, that is all."

The lamplight cast deep shadows on his grandmother's kindly wrinkled face. Her lips puckered as her toothless gums sucked at the bread.

"If your leg is getting better, why is it growing thinner by the day?" she asked. Her strange milky eyes were turned towards him. To Aaron's amazement a tear spilled out and ran down her cheek.

"Thinner?" he repeated stupidly.

Out of the corner of his eye he saw Mother glance warningly at his sisters. Rachel bent over a lamp, Mary fiddled with the hem of her robe. Neither of them looked at him.

A sick feeling poured into his stomach. He shifted his position on the floor and pulled aside his robe. His heart lurched. His left leg looked like a stick. The bones stuck out like knobs on a branch. His right leg was thin too, but compared to it, his bad leg looked ready to wither away and drop off.

Aaron stared at it in horror.

When had it become so thin? And how did Grandmother know what it looked like when she could see only light and shadow? It had been days since he had let her massage it.

Mother was whispering in Grandmother's ear. Aaron pushed aside his supper. He felt sick.

That night Aaron lay sleepless on his pallet. There was a strange new feeling in his left leg. It felt as if it was swelling, yet when he touched it with trembling fingers, it was as thin as ever. For hours Aaron lay still, frozen by panic. He could hear Mark's even breathing. Mary, sleeping over by Rachel, called out in her sleep, making him start. Grandmother snored the night away in her private corner behind the curtain.

At last Aaron fell asleep. He started to dream.

He dreamed he was running down a steep hill. He ran faster and faster. When he tried to stop there was a wrenching feeling in his bad leg. He looked down. The leg had come off and was rolling ahead of him down the hill. All that was left was a bloody stump.

"Aaron? Wake up." Mother was bending over him. "You cried out. Were you having a bad dream?"

He threw his arms around her.

"Oh, Mother, it was horrible. My leg! My leg fell off."

He was afraid to push back the quilt and look in case it was true.

"It was only a dream," she whispered. "Shush now. You will wake Mark. I will stay with you for a while. Tomorrow I will massage your leg with oil. Maybe that will help. When your father comes home we will ask him what is to be done."

Chapter Ten

From that night on, Aaron took no pleasure in village life. He stayed away from the carpenter's shop, the well, and even from Great Uncle Aaron. The cart sat unused outside the door. He didn't want to see or talk to anyone.

Aaron couldn't stop thinking about his leg. Every time he looked at it, it made him think of Peter. He had never really noticed Peter's legs before. Now he thought about them all the time. He couldn't stop comparing them with his own. Did his left leg look as bad? And what about his other leg? Surely it was getting thinner too. Aaron was afraid to go near his friend in case it was true.

All thoughts of his trip to Capernaum and the fun he had had were swept out of his mind. He could think about nothing but the way his legs were wasting away.

Mother massaged them with oil, but it didn't seem to help. Her fingers were much stronger than Grandmother's. She probed and squeezed as if she was trying to pummel some life into them. Once in a while he gave a cry of genuine pain. The rest of the time he felt nothing. When he told Mother she looked more worried than ever.

"You must try to walk," she said. "If you don't use your legs they will wither and die like dead branches."

Dead branches! That was exactly what his left leg looked like now!

She made him stand there and then. To his horror, both legs gave way under him.

"What is happening to them?" he cried, but his mother didn't seem to know.

After that he tried to stand each time he was alone. His right leg felt weak, but most of the time it held him up. There was no feeling in his left leg at all. Aaron was glad the rest of the family couldn't see his trembling attempts to stay on his feet.

At night he lay sleepless on his pallet. Why didn't Father come home? Aaron was sure he would know what to do.

The change in Aaron's brothers and sisters worried Aaron too. Ever since the evening Grandmother had made her comments, they had all avoided him. They treated him as a stranger. John was no longer angry. He was so polite it made Aaron nervous. With the old angry John, at least he knew where he stood. Aaron wished there was some way to find out why John and the others had changed. Day after day he watched John and Mark coming and going with hardly a glance in his direction. Aaron felt sick with despair.

One afternoon Aaron was sitting in the sun

outside the door. He sat facing the street, his back against the sun-warmed mud wall. He was alone. A few minutes earlier John had set out with a hoe over his shoulder. He had gone to the bean field to work until suppertime. Rachel and Mark were out on the hillsides, moving the flock from one pasture to another. Mary was indoors helping Mother.

Aaron pulled down his robe. He felt better when he couldn't see his legs. He leaned his head back and closed his eyes. He could hear voices calling to each other. Someone was hammering. A dog barked. Goats bleated and the bells around their necks tinkled. Children were playing a noisy game across the street.

Closer to home Aaron could hear Grandmother's hens. They clucked happily as they pecked their way through the dust. Mother went past him on her way up to the roof to collect the quilts. She was humming. Grandmother was out of sight around the corner. Aaron could hear her discussing her aches and pains with a neighbor.

Aaron sniffed the sharp-smelling dry air. It smelled of dust and animals and people. It was the smell of home.

Aaron forgot all about his legs for a moment. He raised his arms above his head and stretched with a sigh of pleasure. His robe slipped to one side, exposing his legs. He could feel the warm sun on his ankle. It felt good. He kept his eyes closed and gently moved his foot from side to side. He moved it in circles and bent his knee. His heart started to beat faster. His whole leg felt fine. Maybe it was better!

His mother brushed past him with an armful

of quilts. He waited until she had gone indoors before he opened his eyes. He looked up and down the street. It was empty except for the hens. Holding on to the wall for support, Aaron pulled himself to his feet. When he was sure his good leg would hold him, he put his left foot to the ground. Instantly it started to throb. It was such a shock he almost cried out. He fell against the wall, grazing his elbow. His legs gave way under him and he slid down into the dust.

What was happening now? Why was it throbbing like that?

"Aaron?"

Mary stood in the doorway. Under her arm was an empty water jar. Aaron turned his face away. He didn't want her to see the tears of frustration that filled his eyes.

"I'm going to the well," she said. "Do you want to go with me? I will pull you in the cart."

She stared at him through a tangle of long dark hair. Aaron knew from the way she spoke that she had been told to ask him. He could imagine the whispered instructions "Ask Aaron if he would like to go with you. He has been acting so strangely lately. It will do him good to get out for a while."

"Are you coming, Aaron?" she asked.

"No, thank you," he said abruptly.

"Why not?"

"I don't feel like it."

"But I don't mind pulling you, really I don't."

"I told you I don't want to go with you."

Mary's face clouded over. He could see she was trying not to look hurt. She balanced the water jar on her head, but he was sure she was about to make one more try.

"I bet you can't walk as far as the corner without dropping the jar," he said to get rid of her. "No hands."

Her face cleared. "Of course I can," she said, her black eyes dancing. "Watch."

She did it easily, as Aaron knew she would. At the corner she stopped and gave him a triumphant wave before she disappeared. Minutes later she came racing back.

"Aaron! Aaron!"

Aaron looked up from the picture he was drawing in the dust. He stared in amazement at the flying figure.

"Where is your water jar?" he called. "Whatever happened?"

Chapter Eleven

Mary collapsed onto the bench.

"It's Father," she gasped. "He's home. And guess what he's done. Oh, Aaron, he has bought another donkey!"

She bent over to ease the pain in her side.

"Mother, come quickly," Aaron called. "Father is home."

Mother appeared in the doorway. Her arms were covered to the elbow in flour.

"Oh," she cried. "Look at me!"

She hardly had time to tidy herself before Father came striding down the street. Rachel was close behind him, tugging at the halters of two donkeys.

"I saw Father from the hillside," she called. "Look what he has brought us!"

"The girl has eyes like a hawk," Father's voice boomed out. Aaron leaned forward and watched the tall figure striding towards them. His heart lifted. Father looked like a giant outlined against the sun. Mary's water jar, carried easily in one hand, looked like a toy.

Father stopped in front of Aaron and put down the brimming jar.

"What is this Aaron? You are not at work today?"

"He has had more touble with his leg," Mother explained as he kissed her. "We . . ."

"Joseph? Is that you?" Grandmother appeared around the corner of the house. She walked slowly, guiding herself with one hand on the wall.

"It is me, Mother." Father reached for her and gave her a hug.

"Let go. You will squash all the breath out of me," she protested, but she was smiling.

Father turned back to Aaron.

"Your leg is worse? How can that be?" he asked. His bushy eyebrows shot skyward. "I thought by now you would have forgotten all about it."

"A jar fell on it in the cart on the way home," Grandmother said.

"It looked terrible," said Mother. "It was so swollen and bruised it looked worse than the first time. The swelling went down and you can see the bruises have almost gone, but now it looks as if it is wasting away. What can be wrong with it?"

"Have you tried to walk, Aaron?"

"It won't hold me up when I stand on it."

"How hard have you tried?"

"I've tried a lot. Sometimes there is no feeling in my bad leg and sometimes it throbs and throbs. And now my other leg is getting thinner too and . . . . . ." The panic in Aaron's voice was so real Father put a calming hand on his shoulder.

"Don't upset yourself, my son. Let me look at them."

The big rough hands were gentle.

"Does your leg hurt when I touch it?"

Aaron shook his head.

"Can you move your toes?"

Aaron wriggled them and slowly moved his foot from side to side.

"Good. Now let me see you stand." Father lifted Aaron up. "Put some weight on your leg. That's it. Now, tell me, how does it feel?"

Aaron's only answer was a terrified gasp. Father's bearded face showed no expression as Aaron clung to him.

"It throbs and throbs," Aaron whispered. Sweat was pouring down his face. "It is as if somebody was pounding the bottom of my foot with a hammer."

Father helped him sit down.

"What about your other leg?" he asked.

"It just feels weak."

"I think it is wasting through lack of use," Father said. "Your left leg is a much bigger problem. Maybe something was broken when the jar fell on it. Those jars are heavy. It was mending nicely, so something serious must be hurt deep inside where we can't see it."

Aaron felt so guilty, he didn't dare look up. He was afraid Father would be able to read the truth in his eyes. He didn't relax until Father beckoned the others into the house.

At least John and Mark aren't here, he thought as he watched a handful of sand trickle through his fingers. *But I wonder what Rachel is saying about me.*

To Aaron's surprise, when Father came out again, he was alone and he didn't mention Aaron's legs.

"Your mother wants to prepare a feast for me," he said in his normal cheerful voice. "Come, jump on my back. Let us go for a walk and keep out of the womenfolk's way."

Aaron shinnied up Father's broad back like a one-legged monkey. He wrapped his arms around his father's neck and hugged him.

"Easy! Don't choke me." Father's laugh scattered the hens. "Are you comfortable?"

"Yes," said Aaron. He gave Father one more hug. Now that he was home, Aaron felt as if a great weight had been lifted from his shoulders. *Father is the kind of person who makes you feel safe,* he thought. *Whatever happens to me, I'm glad he is home.*

He straightened his back and looked around. It was amazing how different everything looked from that height. As they walked along he could see over walls and in through the small high house windows. He wondered if he would ever grow to be as tall as Father. John would, you could see that. Mark seemed to have grown the few days they were away in Capernaum. *And me?* Aaron thought. *Will I be tall?* With a sinking heart he remembered his leg. *Whoever heard of a tall, straight one-legged man?*

"Where are we going, Father?" he asked as he tried not to think about it.

"To find your Great Uncle Aaron. Your mother says he will probably be at the house of his old friend Samuel."

Father strode along as if Aaron weighed no

more than a feather. When he turned down an alley, Aaron had to duck to avoid an overhanging thatched roof.

"Ah, but I was afraid of Samuel when I was your age," Father said. "He had such a temper! He was always chasing your uncles and me off his property. The more he chased us, the more we tormented him. We were afraid of him but, like most boys, we enjoyed being scared. How that poor man suffered at our hands! It was years before I found he had a sense of humor. He just didn't like children and we proved him right!"

They crossed a street and cut down another alley. Father called to neighbors and friends with a cheery greeting. He talked on and on, telling stories of his childhood. Aaron had heard most of them before, but he listened with delight.

Outside Samuel's door, Father lowered him down onto a bench.

"I won't be long," he said. "We will go and find your brothers as soon as I have told Uncle Aaron I am home."

As Aaron waited, an ache started deep in his stomach. He was afraid. He didn't want to be there when Father talked to John. What was it John had said about telling him "everything"?

"Why don't you wait until John and Mark come home this evening?" Aaron suggested when they set out again. At least Mother and Grandmother would be there.

"That's not fair, Aaron. Mark knows I am home. He waved to me. And I am sure somebody has told John by now. Besides, I want to look at the animals and the crops. Your brothers have had a lot of responsibility with you sick and me away for such a long time. They have had to work very hard."

"They like to work," Aaron said.

"Not always," Father said over his shoulder. "Do you think they like spending cold nights on windy hillsides? Nobody likes that, Aaron, but somebody has to do it. If work is shared, it is not so bad."

Aaron didn't say anything.

They were out of the village and passing through an olive grove. The path wound uphill to a high point overlooking the valley. At the top Father stopped to get his breath.

"How can you say you like Capernaum better than this?" he demanded. When he turned his head, his beard tickled Aaron's bare arm. "Look at this view and tell me there is anything in a town to compare to this! Every season the hills and valleys of Galilee are beautiful, but in the spring—ah—they make me want to sing God's praises at the top of my voice!"

Chapter Twelve

Below them lay a wide green valley of culti-
vated fields, laced by a silver ribbon of river.
Above the fields a multi-colored haze dusted the
rocky hills. Wildflowers grew in great clumps.
All shades of mauve and purple, orange and yel-
low, were scattered among the fresh green grass.

The patches of bare earth were sand colored.
Here and there across the valley, olive groves
were drab green splotches among the bright
green of the young crops. In the far distance, the
hills were all shades of purple and brown.

Father and Aaron watched birds wheeling
overhead against the clear blue sky.

"It is so beautiful," Father sighed happily.

"Yes it is," Aaron agreed. "But so is the Sea of
Galilee."

"Years ago, maybe," Father said. "Now it is
dead fish and too many people. Have you forgotten the stink so soon?"

Aaron tightened his grip around Father's neck.
"Beauty isn't everything," he argued. "Look how
empty the valley is. It's too quiet for me."

Father shook his head as if he couldn't believe what he was hearing. "Quiet? Listen for a moment before you say it is quiet."

Aaron lifted his head and listened.

Down below, wind rustled through the olive grove. Someone was still hammering down in the village. Children called to each other. Goats bleated. Sheep baaed. Birds sang. And somewhere nearby, a shepherd was playing his pipe.

"Is it Mark?" Aaron asked, and shaded his eyes.

"Can you see him?" Father asked eagerly, and called Mark's name. "Mark! Mark!" His voice echoed back across the valley. The music stopped and there was an answering shout.

"It's Mark," Father said. "How I have missed his cheerful face. I hear he has taken good care of the flock."

Aaron tightened his hold on his father. "I would have helped too if I hadn't hurt myself," he said without thinking.

Father helped Aaron down and looked at him.

"Would you?" he asked.

Aaron concentrated on lowering himself onto a stone wall. He could feel his father's eyes on him, but he didn't look up.

"Why haven't you tried to walk, Aaron?"

Aaron poked a finger at a lizard sunning itself on the wall.

"I—I told you why. At first the pain was too strong, and then, later, my leg went dead."

Their conversation was interrupted by another shout, closer this time. Mark came flying across the rocky slopes, his staff held high. He leaped over the wall and threw himself at Father. It was the old, happy, bright-faced Mark.

"Careful, my son," Father laughed. "We don't want any more accidents in the family."

"I missed you, Father."

"And I you. I hear from your mother that there are four more lambs."

Mark nodded and launched into a description of each birth. Aaron listened as Father asked questions and Mark answered them. Neither of them spoke to him. He sat on the wall, feeling left out and unwanted.

"Your mother is preparing a feast," Father said when talk of the flock was over.

Mark let out a yell of delight and twirled his staff around his head. High up in the hills the sheep baaed, as if in answer. Mark heard them and his face fell. "I have to stay with the flock," he said. "At least until nightfall."

Father put a hand on his shoulder.

"Don't worry about the sheep. The feast is for you, as much as for me. You have earned it. No one is to be missing from the celebration. I will ask if one of your cousins can be spared to keep watch for a few hours."

"I hope there will be plenty of food," Mark grinned. "My stomach is rumbling at the thought of a feast."

Father chuckled. "You know your mother. None of us will go to bed hungry tonight. Come, first we must do some work. I want to see the new lambs. Wait for me here, Aaron. I won't be long."

Aaron felt a stab of jealousy as he watched them go. Father had his arm around Mark's shoulders. They walked in step, deep in conversation.

You had Father to yourself in Capernaum, he reminded himself. *Mark needs him too.*

He stared out over the valley. He tried to see it through Father's eyes. His eyes roamed over the sand colored earth and the patches of bright green, the multi-colored wildflowers and the purple hills. He could see it was beautiful to look at, but to Aaron, that didn't make up for the fact that it was empty of people.

I would much rather be in Capernaum watching the fishing boats coming in, he thought.

Chapter Thirteen

Father spent so much time talking to Mark about the flock, there was no time to go to the fields to find John. Aaron was relieved when Mary came to tell them to hurry home.

The feast started well before sundown.

Mother and Grandmother and Rachel had produced a fine spread in such a short time. There was a large pot of meat and vegetables. There was plenty of bread and olives and goats milk cheese. There was wine and milk to drink. Down the center of the eating mat there were piles of raisins and nuts and dates and dried fig cakes.

Father sat in the place of honor. Mary nestled close beside him and made sure his bowl was never empty. After the meal was over, neighbors and friends dropped by to welcome him home. There was music and singing and there were endless questions. Everybody wanted to hear the news from Capernaum. Father answered them all with great good humor.

Grandmother's questions came first. She

wanted to know all about her nephew Mark. It was years since she had seen him. Their only contact was Father's yearly visit to Capernaum. How was he?

"He is feeling much better," Father told her. "But I worry about him. Since his wife died there is nobody to take care of him. He is lonely, but I don't know if he is lonely enough to marry again." Father's eyes were sad. "If only he had children to comfort him in his old age. How lucky I am to have been so blessed."

He smiled at the circle of faces.

"Talking of children, I have something for each of you," he said. He sent Rachel for a small bulky sack he had left by the door. They waited impatiently while he dug out presents for Mother and Grandmother. "For you, my own dear mother, a pillow stuffed with the finest goose down. Feel how soft it is, I guarantee you will rest better with your head on a pillow like this. For my dear wife, a pair of leather sandals."

He smiled at Mother's delighted face.

"See the workmanship? They were the best in the market. Far better than I could make for you. Now who is next?" He laughed at Mary's excited face. "Mary? Ah yes, here it is. A basket of almond sweetmeats." He bent and kissed the top of her head. "For Rachel, a length of blue cloth. When you have stitched yourself a robe, I hope there will be enough material for you to make one for Mary. In return, maybe she will share her sweetmeats."

Rachel stared wide-eyed at the blue cloth. She felt it, marveling at its softness. "It is nothing like the cloth we weave on our loom," she said. "It is finer by far. Thank you, Father."

Father was laughing at the barely-concealed impatience on the three boys' faces.

"Any guesses what I have bought for you?" he teased.

"No guesses. Please show us," Mark pleaded.

Father handed each of them a small, cloth wrapped bundle. Inside each was an identical knife with a carved handle. They examined their gifts with shining eyes.

"And for you, Father?" Mary said. "What did you buy for yourself?"

"Me? A sack of dried fish," he answered. "Don't look so disgusted. I love fish. Every day in Capernaum I ate fresh fish from the Sea of Galilee. Right, Aaron? And then there is the donkey. The fleeces fetched a fair price. Now that our flock produces enough wool for ourselves and to sell, maybe I can buy other things."

"We will need to build a stable now that we have two donkeys," John said. "Where shall we put it?"

Aaron watched him uneasily. So far Father hadn't had any time alone with John, but it couldn't last. Aaron dreaded the thought of what tomorrow might bring.

"That is enough talk of work for today," Mother said. "Tell us about Capernaum, Joseph. What did you see there?"

"Aaron saw more than I did," he answered. "Surely he has told you all about it."

"He told me," Mary said. It was hard for Aaron to keep calm with John and Mark and Rachel staring at him.

"You tell us, Father," Rachel said. "Tell us

about the people."

"What is there to tell? That there are too many?" Father joked.

"What are they like?" Mark asked.

"There are all kinds. Rich and poor."

"Tell us about the rich ones," Rachel said.

"They are richer by far than anyone in our village. They are merchants and tax collectors and the like. And there are Romans. There is a small camp outside the town. They often pass through Capernaum on their way to the town of Tiberias. They say the Romans there live like kings! They have houses with many rooms and water that flows out of pipes. One day Aaron and I saw one of their women being carried through the fish market. Rich Roman women never walk. They are carried around like useless ornaments. No wonder they have such lilywhite skin." He reached over and picked up Rachel's work-roughened, sunburnt hand. "Look at this. This is a hand to be proud of!"

Before Rachel could stop him, he had raised her hand to his mouth and given it a kiss. As the boys nudged each other and laughed, she blushed and snatched her hand away.

"Don't do that, Father," she said, but she was laughing too. "Tell us more about the Roman woman. What was she wearing?"

Father's eyes flashed and his beard jutted out.

"Do you think I cared enough to notice what she was wearing? Or any of them? Parasites! They act as if they own the land, our land. They bleed it dry with their tax collectors. Robbers, they are, robbers of the worst kind."

"Enough of such talk, Joseph," Grandmother

said. "Tell us, what is the news from the synagogue?"

"The talk is all of Jesus of Nazareth."

Father looked at their blank faces.

"Didn't Aaron tell you about the famous Rabbi?
The carpenter's son?"

"A carpenter's son?" Mother echoed. "What is
so special about him?"

"He can work miracles. He can cure people.
Drive out devils. Sometimes he touches the sick
people. Sometimes he just speaks to them. Aaron
was outside a house when Jesus cured a paralyzed man. Aaron said the man was lowered
through the roof. A short time later this same
man walked out of the house carrying the bed."

"He told us nothing of that," Grandmother
said.

Father stared at Aaron in amazement.

"Why didn't you tell them, Aaron? It was all
you talked about that night."

"I—I forgot," Aaron mumbled, his face red.
"There was so much else to tell."

"Everyone is talking about Jesus of Nazareth,"
Father went on. "I heard him preach at the syn-
agogue." He paused and looked from face to face.
"I saw him cure some people."

Aaron's heart lurched.

"You saw him?" Mary gasped. "What happened?"

Father took a sip of wine and drew her closer.
He was enjoying himself hugely.

"One day I was down by the edge of the sea
with Cousin Mark. He was feeling better, and I
thought the fresh air would do him good. We
came upon a crowd gathered at the water's edge.

Naturally we stopped to ask why they were there. Someone told us the Rabbi Jesus was preaching and healing people. One man openly called him the Messiah." Father paused to toss a fistful of raisins into his mouth.

"The Messiah?" Grandmother gasped.

"Go on, Joseph," Mother urged.

"What happened?" Rachel whispered. Her eyes were like great dark pools.

"It was the most wonderful thing I have ever seen. Jesus and his followers were in a boat a few lengths from the beach. A man was screaming and crying and throwing himself in the water. It took two men to hold him. They said he was possessed. I was too far away to hear what the Rabbi said to him, but suddenly the man grew quiet. His friends helped him out of the water and he was walking like anyone else. His whole face changed. He was at peace. Anyone could see it. As he went away he was praising God while his friends wept with joy."

"I wish I had been there," Mark said.

"What did the Rabbi talk about?" John asked.

"Wonderful things. He told stories. Even your Great Uncle Aaron couldn't match them. He talked about love and forgiving your neighbor. And about God and Heaven and what we must do to earn a place there."

In the silence that followed, Grandmother sighed.

"It was very strange," Father went on. "I was only one in a crowd and yet I felt as if Jesus was speaking only to me. Afterwards, other people said the same. It was as if he knew what was in every man's heart."

Aaron felt a shiver go down his spine.

"Tell us more," Mark pleaded.

"Another time, when I heard him preach in the synagogue, he healed a man's withered hand. There were some who grumbled and said he was breaking the law because it was the Sabbath. They wanted to lay a complaint against him, but the look of joy on the man's face was enough for me! When he left the synagogue he held his hand high so all could see it. He praised God at the top of his voice, and so did I."

Mother sighed.

"It is a truly wonderful thing," she said. "I wonder if the rest of us will ever have the chance to hear him preach." She put her hand on Grandmother's arm. "Wouldn't you like to hear him, Mother? You could ask him to give you back your sight."

Grandmother shook her head.

"I am too old," she said. "I have seen all I need to see. I have my memories. No, if I saw the Rabbi Jesus, I would go to him and ask him to give Aaron back the use of his leg."

Everyone stared at Aaron. A wave of red flooded his face. He hung his head, hoping it wouldn't show in the lamplight. He busied himself examining his knife. He prayed somebody would change the subject, before John said something.

It was Father who spoke first. He stretched and gave a giant yawn.

"I am tired," he said. "It was a long journey and I am ready for bed. We have a lot of work to do tomorrow. Mary, you and Rachel help your mother clear away the leftover food. Mark, see to it the donkeys are fed before you go to bed. Aaron, to bed with you."

Father walked John to the door.

"This will be your last watch for a while, my son," he told him. "You have my promise. Don't forget to thank your cousins for their help." He put his hand on John's shoulder. "May God watch over you this night."

Aaron was glad to get out of everybody's way. He unrolled his pallet and lay down. He was still holding his knife when he pulled the goatskin up around his shoulders.

The thought of the morning filled him with dread. He tried to stay awake. He wanted the night to last as long as possible. He tried to keep his eyes open, but it had been a long day.

By the time Mother blew out the lamps, Aaron was sound asleep.

Chapter Fourteen

Aaron went back to watching the sheep next morning. Father carried him out to the pasture on his back. While Aaron kept watch over the newborn lambs in a fold in the hills, Father and John checked the rest of the flock.

"Call us if you need us," Father said.

Aaron sat under a tree and watched John anxiously. He was too far away to be able to hear what he was saying. He seemed to be talking about the flock, but was he? Aaron watched and waited.

The sun was high in the sky before they were finished. Father walked over and joined Aaron in the shade. He wiped the sweat from his face and picked up the water bag. Aaron waited for the lecture he was sure was coming. Father said, "John will be thirsty too," and took the bag and left.

John is bound to tell him now, Aaron thought. *The work is done and there will be time for them to talk of other things.*

Father and John sat down on a rock. Their

backs were to Aaron. They didn't seem to be talking, but it was hard to tell.

The uncertainty was making Aaron nervous.

If only I could walk, he thought. *If only I could get up and move around. If only I didn't have to sit here, waiting.*

When it was time to eat, John was still there.

Why doesn't he go home? Aaron thought.

It was John who came to collect Father's share of the food. He divided the bread and cheese into two portions without saying a word. As he turned to leave, Aaron said, "John?"

"What is it?"

"What—what did you tell Father?" Aaron's heart was pounding.

"About what?"

"About my accident."

"You mean when you fell down the hillside?" John asked.

"No," Aaron gulped. His face was burning. "The other one. The jar . . . . ." Should he tell John the truth and get it over with?

John stared down at him. There was no anger in his eyes, only pity. Aaron couldn't understand it. What had made his brother change?

"The jar was an accident? I don't think so, Aaron. At first, I admit I thought it was. That was why I was angry with you. I thought you were using it as an excuse to get out of going back to work. I see now I was mistaken."

"You were?" Aaron said faintly.

"Yes. I see now it was a punishment from God."

Aaron shook his head to clear it. What was John talking about? "I don't understand, John.

What do you mean by saying the jar was a punishment?"

"It was a punishment for tricking the rest of us. For pretending after you fell rescuing Mary that your ankle wasn't getting better so that Father would take you to Capernaum."

Aaron's mouth fell open.

"God punished you by making the jar fall on you so you can't walk at all."

Aaron wanted to shout "You have it all wrong! I never *dreamed* Father would take me with him. It was as much a surprise to me as it was to you. I just wanted to put off going back to work, that's all. It had nothing to do with Capernaum!"

A feeling of helplessness had drained all his strength away. *John's mind is already made up,* he thought. *I can tell.* "I didn't know Father was going to take me with him," he protested weakly.

"Of course you didn't *know,*" John said. "But you hoped."

"I didn't! It never crossed my mind. Not once."

It was clear his brother didn't believe him.

"Do you deny telling Mark you wished we lived in Capernaum?"

"No, I—I don't deny it, but . . ."

"Are we wrong believing that you hate watching sheep above anything else?"

"No, but I am not guilty of what you say!"

It was like being in the middle of a nightmare.

Aaron decided he'd better tell the truth now, before it gets any worse. "The jar didn't really fall on me," he cried. "I made it up. God didn't punish me because it never happened."

"Then where did the bruises come from? And the swelling?"

"The jars broke loose and rolled against my ankle while I was asleep. It looked awful, but it didn't hurt much."

"Then why can't you walk?"

"I could if I tried!" Aaron cried desperately. He caught hold of the tree trunk and pulled himself to his feet. Both legs buckled under him and he fell into John's arms.

"I could walk before," he sobbed as John helped him sit down. "I don't know why I can't walk now."

"Don't you?" John asked. "Oh Aaron, tell the truth for once."

Aaron sat in a stunned silence after John had gone. One thing was clear. The reason John and Mark and Rachel had been avoiding him. They thought God was punishing him for tricking Father into taking him to Capernaum. It was almost funny.

Maybe God is punishing me, Aaron thought with a shiver. *But not for that. Maybe he is punishing me for lying. Why, oh why did I lie about the jar?*

That night Father rearranged the watches.

"You and I will take the night watch, Aaron," he said. "John can become a farmer for a few days. Rachel has been doing most of the field work, so she can help Mark with the day watch."

Everyone was pleased with the changes, even Aaron. He had dreaded being put on watch with John. Ever since the conversation he had avoided John. One question came back to him again and again. Was God punishing him for lying about the jar? Whenever he tried to stand and his legs wouldn't obey him, he was sick with worry.

Even in Father's cheerful company, the night watches were endless. It was always cold out on the open hillsides. The kind of late spring cold that is damp and gets inside your bones. Being unable to walk made it much harder to bear. Father could move around to keep warm. Aaron had to sit and shiver in the chilly wind.

It was the duty of the day watch to gather enough fuel for the night watch's fire. Aaron's job was to light the fire and keep it burning during the coldest hours. Those hours, when the two of them sat close to the flames, kept the nights from being unbearable. It was then that Father told his stories, his voice filling the darkness, his laughter driving away Aaron's fears.

Each night they took turns sleeping for awhile. "Wake me if anything disturbs the flock," Father always said. While Father slept, Aaron sat bolt upright and listened until the blood hummed in his ears. He crouched so close to the fire his cloak was often singed. His eyes strained to pierce the velvety darkness on cloudy nights. When it was windy, there were all kinds of strange noises. The wind made the fire burn so brightly the fuel was soon used up. Aaron didn't understand how Father could sleep so soundly. He ached with cold and fear and shivered underneath his cloak. He thought of his brothers asleep in their warm beds. He remembered how John had taken the night watch alone, night after night, with never a break.

No wonder John was angry with me, Aaron thought with sudden understanding.

After three nights, Aaron changed watches with Mark, and shared the day watch with

Rachel. He rode to and from the hillsides on one of the donkeys. Aaron liked the day watch far better. Rachel never bothered him. She liked to wander off and gaze out over the valley. For her, it was a pleasant change to have nothing much to do. At home she was always busy, and the crops took constant care. Out on the grassy rock strewn slopes she had time to pick wildflowers. She made crowns of flowers for the lambs and played with them for hours.

Aaron thought about Capernaum as he watched the flock. He thought with longing of the busy market, the crowded streets and the waterfront. He thought about Benjamin too, and his life on the fishing boats.

One day he said to Rachel, "I am going to ask Father if he will let me be something else, instead of a shepherd."

Rachel was unpacking their midday meal. She looked up and said, "What do you want to be?"

"Before I went to Capernaum I wanted to be a carpenter," he said. "But now I think I'd like to be a fisherman."

"A fisherman? What does our family know about fishing?" Rachel asked. "Besides, whoever heard of a fisherman who can't walk? A carpenter, that is different. You can make things sitting down. If Peter can be a carpenter, so can you."

She said it in such a matter-of-fact way, Aaron stared at her in horror.

"Are you saying I won't ever walk again?" he cried. "Of course I will! My leg will get better."

"When?"

"I don't know when!" They were sitting in the shade but Aaron could feel the sweat running down his face. "I'm not like Peter. I'm not really crippled."

"You weren't crippled when you were in Capernaum," she agreed. "Father says you walked everywhere with no more than a limp. He says that is why he sent you home. You weren't crippled until the jar fell on you. John says . . . ."

"The jar *didn't* fall on me! I made it up. I told John I made it up." Aaron was shouting so loudly the nearest sheep bumped into each other in fright. Rachel had to call to them to calm them down.

"Oh Aaron," she sighed. "Bruises all colors of the rainbow didn't come from your imagination. John says God was punishing you. I think he is right."

Aaron felt hollow. As if all the air had been sucked out of him. "He's not right," he gasped. "It's not true."

Aaron felt sick. He couldn't bear to look at the food Rachel had placed in front of him. What if John was partly right? What if God had been watching when he made up those stories about his leg, and had decided he had to be taught a lesson? Only not, as John thought, by making a jar fall on his bad ankle. But by taking away the use of his legs, bit by bit, until he couldn't walk at all.

Maybe I do deserve to be punished, Aaron thought. But not that much! Never to walk again? Would God really go that far?

It was as if Rachel could read his mind.

"You may be able to fool Mother and Grandmother, but you can't fool God, Aaron," she said quietly. "He sees everything. You can't fool

Father either. He knows what you are up to."

"What did you tell him?"

"Nothing. We talked about it and decided to say nothing. I can tell by the way Father looks at you that he has his suspicions." She paused and shrugged. "You are in God's hands now, Aaron."

Aaron stared blindly out over the valley.

He had never dreamed his pretending would lead to this. He would be like Peter for the rest of his life—half a man, hopping around, unable to run and jump or even walk. It wasn't fair! He hadn't done anything terrible. He hadn't hurt anybody, or stolen anything or . . . or cheated. He bit his lip to stop himself from crying.

He *had* cheated. He had cheated his brothers out of their free time, and Rachel too. And he had cheated Mother and Grandmother by making them believe he was in pain when he wasn't.

If my leg ever gets better I am going to run away, he told himself wildly. He gazed at the distant hills. *I will go as far away from here as possible. To Jerusalem, maybe! Anywhere, just as long as it is a place where nobody knows me.*

But God will know you, a voice inside him said.

Chapter Fifteen

That evening, when Mark arrived to take over the watch, Aaron could tell something exciting had happened.

"What is it?" he asked.

"Wait and see," Mark grinned.

"Tell us," urged Rachel.

"You will find out soon enough."

Rachel ran to untether the donkey, and she and Aaron hurried home.

There was a large crowd at the well. A woman called to them as they passed by.

"Have you heard the news? Jesus of Nazareth will be passing this way. He is going to stop and preach to us."

Aaron felt a jab of fear. In Capernaum he had wanted more than anything to hear the famous preacher speak. Now he was afraid to go near him.

Rachel, walking alongside the donkey, said, "I can't wait! To think he is coming here after all Father said about him. I hope nothing happens to make him change his mind."

I hope something does, thought Aaron.

At supper, the talk was all of the unexpected visit.

"It is wonderful news," Father said. Now you will have the chance to hear him for yourselves."

"Maybe we will see a miracle," said Rachel.

"Wouldn't it be wonderful?" Mother said. "I hear he is going to preach on a hillside outside the village. They say people will be coming from all over the countryside. They are expecting huge crowds."

"When will he be here?" Grandmother asked.

"In two days."

"Oh Mother, may we go and hear him?" Rachel pleaded.

"Of course. We will all go."

"Somebody will have to watch the sheep," said the practical John.

"I'll do it," Aaron offered.

"No, Aaron, I will keep watch," Father said. "I want all of you to hear the Rabbi preach. It may be your only chance."

Grandmother leaned forward. "It is wonderful news, Joseph. We must find out what time he will arrive. We must be there early so Aaron and I can find a place at the front of the crowd. I want to be close enough to speak to him afterwards."

She groped for Aaron's hand and squeezed it. Aaron stared at her with a sense of foreboding.

"Are you going to ask him for your eyesight, Grandmother?" Rachel asked.

"Of course not! I told you at the feast what I would do if I met him. Do you think I would ask for myself when Aaron cannot walk? What a short memory you have, Rachel."

Aaron pulled his hand free. He hoped Grandmother hadn't felt it tremble. "I don't mind watching the sheep while the rest of you go," he said in desperation.

"You must be there, Aaron," Mother said firmly.

Grandmother nodded. "I hope he will have time to listen to me," she said. "There will be so many people wanting his help. That is why we must be sitting close to him, Aaron. When he sees your legs he will surely help you."

Aaron felt like a trapped animal. *There must be some way out!* he thought.

"How can I go with you?" He tried to keep his voice normal. "If he preaches on the hillsides I won't have any way to get there."

"Of course you will. We have two donkeys now," Mother reminded him. "Your grandmother can ride one, and you can ride the other."

"But what about you?"

She laughed. "Me? I am not so old that I can't walk over the countryside. I can still climb the hills without help."

Father got up to go and join Mark on the night watch. As he tucked his sling and his club in his belt he stared at Aaron. He had a strange expression on his face. He looked as if he was disappointed by what he saw.

Over the next two days, Aaron hardly spoke to anyone. On watch with Rachel, he kept to himself as much as possible. He wanted to be left alone with his fear and his panic.

Surely there must be some way out of the trouble he was in. There must be! Father had said Jesus of Nazareth was known for being able to see into men's hearts. Benjamin had said the same thing.

If he can see inside me he will know what I have done, Aaron reasoned. *He will know all about God punishing me. What if he picks me out of the crowd and points at me and tells everyone?*

Aaron knew how the rest of his family would feel. He could imagine the shock to Mother and Grandmother. And then there was Father. What would he say when he heard about it? Father had a lot of family pride. Aaron was sure he would never be forgiven.

If only I could run away! he thought.

When he was alone, he forced himself to stand. He managed to stay on his feet as long as there was something to hold on to. But as soon as he tried to walk, his legs gave way under him.

There was no escape, and Aaron was terrified.

Tell Father, a voice inside him said. *Tell Father everything and ask him to help you.*

Father doesn't really care, another voice said. *If he did he would see how upset you are and ask you why.*

When they were together, Aaron tried to will his father into saying, "What is wrong, Aaron?"

If he says that I will tell him everything, Aaron vowed. He waited, sick with hope, but nothing happened. Father talked about the crops and the flock and the times he had seen the Rabbi Jesus in Capernaum, He didn't seem to notice that anything was wrong and Mother put down Aaron's pale face and lack of appetite to excitement.

The day of the visit dawned bright and clear. John had had the night watch. By the time Father left the house to relieve him, people were streaming into the village. Some of them stopped at the door to ask the way to the place where Jesus was to preach. Grandmother heard the passing feet and started to worry.

"It is time to go," she said.

"Jesus is walking from Cana. He won't be here yet," Mother said. "He isn't due to speak until the sun is overhead."

"I know, but we must get a good place at the front," Grandmother insisted. "And Rachel must sit with us. I will need her help over the rough ground when I go to speak to the Rabbi."

Aaron's hands were clammy with fear. For two days he had hoped he would fall ill. He had lain awake at night as he tried to will himself into a fever. Every time he closed his eyes he could see the whole terrible scene in his mind.

Grandmother would point him out. Jesus would look at him. Straightaway he would know what Aaron had done. Just last night Father had said again that some people thought Jesus had been sent by God. Someone like that would know all about Aaron's sins.

The Rabbi would tell everyone why God had punished Aaron. He would be shamed before the whole world. People would point him out. Children would jeer and make fun. The family would be disgraced too. The thought filled Aaron with dread.

For two days he had hoped and prayed something would happen to save him. Now it was too late.

Aaron saw the people passing the door. There were more and more of them every minute. Aaron watched them and swore he would never go anywhere near the preacher from Nazareth.

I can't run away, he thought. *The only thing I can do is hide until he has gone.*

Chapter Sixteen

There was only one place to hide inside the house. It was the storage area under the sleeping platform. The difficulty would be getting into it without being seen. Aaron hoped that in the confusion of leaving, each person would think he had gone with somebody else. By the time they found out their mistake, it would be too late.

Aaron sat on the edge of the platform. As he waited, he forced himself to keep calm. The rest of the family were too busy to notice him. John was not yet home. Mark had gone to fetch the donkeys. Mary had been sent to the well to fill two water bags. Mother disappeared behind the curtain to brush Grandmother's hair. Only Rachel was left. She was wrapping bread and some olives in a cloth to take with them.

Aaron rubbed his sweating palms on his robe as he waited for her to turn her back. At last the moment came. She bent over the olive jar. Swiftly and silently Aaron lowered himself to the floor, and wriggled in among the rolled eating mats and the cooking pots. He dragged his legs out of sight just as Rachel said, "Mother?"

Aaron's heart was pounding so loudly, he felt sure Rachel could hear it.

"Yes, Rachel?" Mother said.

"Should I wrap some cheese, too?"

"Child, we are not going there to eat! Come now. Bread and olives will be plenty."

As footsteps crossed the platform above his head, Aaron wriggled further away from the opening. Pressed against the rear wall in the pitch dark, he felt safe.

The air was stuffy and hot in that confined space. The footsteps had dislodged some dried mud and dust. Aaron rubbed the end of his nose to stop a sneeze.

He could hear Grandmother's slow uncertain tread just above his head.

"Is everyone ready?" She sounded impatient.

"I think so," Mother said. "Where is Aaron?"

"I am sure he was here just now," Rachel told her. "He must be outside with Mark."

Aaron heard them leave. Then there was silence, broken only by the anxious thumping of his heart.

"We can't leave without him." It was Mother's voice. She sounded as if she was standing in the doorway. "I wonder where . . . . oh, there's John. Tell him we are ready to go, but we can't find Aaron."

"We had better not delay much longer." It was Mark's voice. "I have never seen so many people, and they are still coming."

Two sets of footsteps sounded inside the house.

"Why don't the rest of you go?" John's voice

said. Aaron held his breath and listened. "As soon as I've washed and eaten some breakfast, I'll look for him. His cart is outside the door so he can't have gone far. Leave one of the donkeys, and I'll bring him with me."

"Don't be too long," were Mother's parting words. Aaron's heart sank as he listened to the goodbyes.

It was so hot under the sleeping platform he was starting to sweat. He wiped his face and listened to John walking around. *Go!* he urged him silently. *Leave before I suffocate!*

Aaron could hear water being poured, and some splashing sounds. He was thinking of a cool drink and how good it would taste, when John suddenly leaped up onto the platform. He landed heavily and started to stamp his feet. The air in the storage space filled with dust. Aaron closed his eyes and held his breath. He started to cough and then he sneezed.

There was the silence above his head. Suddenly the eating mats were pulled roughly aside. John's face appeared in the opening, outlined against the light.

"I knew you were under there." John's staff poked Aaron in the stomach. "Come out, Aaron. We are late."

Aaron spat the dust from his mouth and wiped his streaming eyes. "I'm not going."

"Oh yes you are. Come out before I drag you out."

"I said I'm not going!"

The end of the staff poked him again. It hurt and Aaron winced. He wondered how long he could hold out.

"Why are you hiding, Aaron? Are you afraid the Rabbi will recognize you for the trickster you are?"

"I don't know what you are talking about."

"Don't you? Look Aaron, I am trying to be understanding. I'm trying very hard. Don't make me drag you out by the hair on your head."

The staff poked him again, in the chest this time.

"Go away, John," Aaron started to cough again. "You can do anything. I don't care. I still won't go, and you can't make me!"

"Why won't you go?"

"Because."

"Because what? I won't go away until you tell me."

"Because . . . . . all right then! I'll tell you why. I don't want to be there when Grandmother speaks to Jesus about me. I—I'm afraid of what he might say."

To Aaron's surprise, John withdrew his staff. "Why, Aaron?"

"Because i-if he is sent from God, he will know what I have done."

John stared at him.

"What *have* you done, Aaron? The truth this time.

"I told you before. You wouldn't believe me."

"Tell me again. Everything."

Aaron told him. When he had finished, John grunted and said, "I believe you. You are in a lot of trouble Aaron, and you have brought it on yourself. But you are my brother. I don't want to see you shamed before our neighbors. I love you even if you do hate sheep!" He flashed a grin into the darkness. "Listen. I'm going now. I will tell Mother I couldn't find you."

His face disappeared.

"Thanks," Aaron called, his voice weak with relief. "Could you stop Grandmother from talking to Jesus? Please, John?"

"No, Aaron. Nobody can stop Grandmother except you."

Aaron groaned.

"I wish none of it had ever happened. I wish . . . ."

"There is no point in wishing," John said. "Cheer up. It could be a lot worse. At least you won't be there to see what happens."

Chapter Seventeen

Aaron waited until John had gone before he came out of his hiding place. He was hot and sticky and covered with dust, but he didn't have the energy to move. When he finally crawled, blinking, out into the light, he stretched out on the cool dirt floor for a few minutes.

Thirst drove him over to the water jar by the door. Outside, he breathed in the fresh air and looked around. The village seemed to be asleep, it was so empty. The sun was above the rooftops. Aaron could tell by its position that it would soon be time for the Rabbi's sermon to begin. His stomach ached at the thought.

From the hills to the south of the village came the hum of many voices. It sounded as if the whole world was there. The hum rose and fell. The village, by contrast, was silent. The clucking of hens and the bleating of tethered goats were the only sounds. Aaron had never seen it so deserted.

He leaned his back against the mud wall and closed his eyes. He felt strangely weak, as if he had given every ounce of energy in trying to hide, and now he had nothing left. The hum lulled him until, suddenly, it rose to a roar. The roar could mean only one thing. Jesus of Nazareth had arrived.

Without knowing why, Aaron thought of Peter. He knew Peter and his family had gone to hear Jesus. He had seen them pass the house. Peter had ridden by on a donkey. His face was full of hope.

Aaron couldn't get Peter's face out of his mind. Was he going to hear the Rabbi, hoping for a miracle?

"It is Peter who needs his help, not me," Aaron said out loud. "Grandmother should ask Jesus to help Peter. If it wasn't for me, maybe she would."

It was the truth, and he could see it clearly. It made him feel terrible. For the first time he thought of the other sick people in the village. The wife of Jacob had given birth to a sick baby that wasn't expected to live. Ruth, his mother's friend had sickness in her house. Her husband had died, and now one of her children had caught the fever. Then there was Old Benjamin with his hunched back, and the boy who was blind.

And then there was Grandmother.

If it wasn't for me, she might ask for her eyesight. She would like that, I know she would, even though she says she doesn't care. Nobody can enjoy being blind.

As Aaron sat, alone and miserable, outside the door, a thought at the back of his mind kept trying to push itself forward.

It is up to you. Nobody can stop Grandmother except you, Aaron. John's words echoed inside his head.

It is up to you. The words were repeated again and again.

Aaron didn't want to listen.

There must be some other way! he thought in desperation. *There must be somebody who would help me. Father? Yes! That's it! Father will help me.*

"I will go to him and ask him to stop Grandmother," he said out loud. "I will confess everything and ask him to help me. When he hears what I have done he will understand why Grandmother must be stopped. If I hurry, there will be time. I can watch the flock until he gets back."

It never occurred to Aaron that his father might refuse to go. If it meant somebody else would have the chance to be cured, he was sure Father would do it.

Now that he had come to a decision, Aaron felt a burst of energy. He reached inside the door for his staff. John had left the donkey tied under the shade of the grapevine. Aaron crawled over and scrambled up onto its back.

As the donkey trotted through the deserted village, Aaron realized the hum had stopped. The silence meant Jesus must have already started to preach. He urged the donkey to go faster.

"Keep calm" he told himself. "When you start to tell Father, don't panic, otherwise he won't understand. You will waste valuable time explaining, and he may be too late to stop her."

His resolution lasted until he saw the flock and heard his father's surprised shout.

"Aaron? What are you doing here?"

"Father . . . please . . . you must stop Grandmother!" The words tripped over each other. "Peter . . . . it's Peter who needs the miracle, not me. Peter. You must . . . . Grandmother. What about her eyes? *Please* stop her."

Father came running and caught hold of the reins.

"I don't understand a word you are saying. Why are you here? You are supposed to be with the rest of the family. I wanted you to hear the Rabbi Jesus preach. Calm down, my son, and explain yourself. Take your time."

"There is no time!" Aaron cried. "You must stop Grandmother."

"From what?"

"From speaking to Jesus about me."

"Why, Aaron? Why should I stop her?" Father's steady eyes seemed to be looking inside him. "Tell me, my son."

"Because I tricked everyone into thinking my ankle was bad when it wasn't," he whispered. "I am sorry I did it. I wish . . ."

The whole story came tumbling out. From time to time Father stopped him, and asked a question. But when Aaron had finished, Father didn't say a word.

"That's why you must stop her, Father. Please go and make her ask for a miracle for somebody else."

"No, Aaron."

Aaron thought he had misheard.

"There isn't much time, Father."

"I told you no."

Aaron couldn't believe it. He was sure that

once he confessed and said he was sorry, Father would help him.

"Please," he pleaded. "I am willing to take God's punishment for what I've done."

"God isn't punishing you, Aaron," Father said quietly.

"But I can't walk at all now. John told me . . . ."

"That God had done it to punish you? He was wrong, Aaron. God doesn't punish people by crippling them. You have brought this on yourself."

"How?"

"By not using your legs. If I pen an animal so it cannot move it will lose the power of its legs. Not overnight, but little by little. By deciding to stop trying to walk you brought about the same result. God gave you your legs so you could walk. If you don't walk on them, they will wither away as surely as an animal's legs."

Aaron frowned as he tried to understand.

"I told you your right leg was weak through lack of use," Father said. "That was when I thought the jar had fallen on the other one. You tell me now you made that up. If I had known the truth I would have said the same thing about your left leg."

"You mean it was the same for both of them?"

"Yes. Your bad leg was getting better when I sent you home, wasn't it?"

Aaron nodded.

"That was because you had started to use it again. Every day while we were in Capernaum you tried to walk on it. But as soon as you got home, you stopped. This time your good leg wasn't used either because you had Peter's cart to ride in. You have lost the power to walk not because God is punishing you, but because you acted the part of the cripple too well."

Aaron shuddered. Hadn't John called him "a little play actor"?

"I couldn't bear to look at my legs," he said in a low voice. "I still can't. I have nightmares about them. Oh Father, I am so afraid."

"I know, my son. I have watched your suffering. As your Father I wanted to spare you, but I could not. If God is punishing you, Aaron, it is not by taking away the use of your legs but working there, inside your head." He put a comforting hand on Aaron's curly hair. "Until you are truly sorry for what you have done, there will be no peace for you."

"But I am! I am sorry!"

"Good. Then you must go to your grandmother and make things right."

"I can't," Aaron wept. "Not in front of all those people. What if she won't listen to me?"

"You must make her listen."

"I can't do it, Father. I'm afraid. Afraid of what Jesus will say."

"You must conquer that fear, Aaron. You have come this far. Don't give up now. The struggle inside you is inside all of us. It is your struggle that Jesus of Nazareth talks about. The fight between good and evil. You of all my sons have the strength to win that struggle."

"Me? I don't understand."

"You are a boy with powerful feelings, Aaron. You can use these feelings to do good things as well as bad. It is up to you. Each man must fight the battle for himself."

"I'm not a man," Aaron cried.

"I know." Father grasped him by the shoulders and kissed him on the cheek. "You are a boy, but you will soon be a man, Aaron. Now is the time to find out what kind of man you will be. Don't fail me, for I have all kinds of plans for you."

Father turned the donkey around and pointed up the hill.

"Go that way. It isn't far. I have been listening to the crowd. It is silent now so the Rabbi Jesus must be speaking. Hurry."

Father slapped the donkey to start it on its way. As Aaron guided it up the hill, the thoughts were tumbling around in his head. What had Father meant when he said "You of all my sons have the strength"? He had looked proud when he said it. There had been love in his eyes. Aaron shook his head in wonder. He had confessed something that he was sure would make his father hate him, and Father had looked at him with love. And what had he meant by "all kinds of plans"? What plans?"

At the top, Aaron looked back.

Father was standing near the flock. In one hand he held his staff. The other was raised to shade his eyes as he watched Aaron ride away. From that distance he looked like any other shepherd. Aaron knew differently. Even as he wanted to hate his father for not taking the burden from him, his heart swelled with love.

For the first time in his life Aaron looked at the peaceful scene with longing.

Chapter Eighteen

It took Aaron only a few minutes to reach the place where Jesus was preaching. People were crowded as thick as flies on the sides of the bowl-shaped dip in the hills. Here and there a child cried or a sick person called out, but mostly there was silence. Everyone's attention was on a small rise of land down below.

A man was standing on a rock. He was speaking slowly and clearly, turning so that everybody could hear him.

Aaron reined in the donkey at the edge of the crowd. He was too far away to see the man's face clearly but he listened to his voice. It was just as his father had said. Even when the man turned away to talk to the people behind him, Aaron had the feeling the words were meant for him alone.

"You must love your neighbor as yourself."

"Love your neighbor as yourself," Aaron repeated under his breath.

Aaron thought of Peter, his neighbor, his friend. Peter had never been able to run over the hillsides. He had never walked to the well, or to a friend's house. If he wanted to go anywhere by himself, he had to crawl through the dust. Aaron had only done it once, but it had been enough for him. He had sworn he would never crawl anywhere again. Peter didn't have a choice.

"If I loved Peter as much as I love myself, I would do anything to help him," Aaron said to himself. "I wouldn't worry what people might think of me. I wouldn't care if Jesus told the whole world just as long as Peter was cured."

I must do something, he thought, but when he looked at the huge crowd, his courage failed him.

"Always treat others as you would like them to treat you," the Rabbi was saying.

Aaron heard, and his face burned with shame. If John or Mark had done what he had done, how would he feel?

"I would hate them if they tricked me like I tricked them," he said with feeling. He thought of the morning when John had tried to get him up. Mark had been wanting to go to market for a long time. He had asked for one short break from watching the sheep. It wasn't much to ask after all the hours of extra work he had done.

How could I have been so selfish? Aaron thought, as he remembered how he had let Mother tell Mark he couldn't go.

As he thought of his brothers, his eyes scanned the crowd. Where were they? With a stab of panic, Aaron realized how hard it would be to find them.

There was no time to lose. There was no time to listen to the rest of the words Aaron was sure were directed at him.

"Find Grandmother and stop her," he urged himself. "You must do it for Peter."

Seated nearby were some people from the village.

"Have you seen my family?" he asked them.

They shook their heads. Aaron shaded his eyes and scanned the faces of the people sitting closest to the rock. From this distance it was impossible to recognize anyone in the tightly packed crowd.

Aaron knew how determined his grandmother could be.

They must be down there somewhere, he thought.

He rode around to where the crowd was the thinnest. He slid to the ground and tied the donkey to a thorn bush. There was only one way for him to get down to the rock, and that was sitting down. From long practice Aaron had learned to move quite fast. He eased himself past the first cluster of people. He wriggled his way around some rocks and bushes and on down the slope. Now and again somebody would move to let him by, or hold out a hand to help him. Most of the people seemed unaware that he was trying to get by. They were listening, spellbound to the words of the man on the rock.

It was a long and painful journey for Aaron. The ground was rough. In steep places he had to use his staff as a brake. The detours he had to make made the way a lot longer. Whenever he stopped to rest for a moment, he looked for a familiar face in the crowd but saw no one he knew.

Several times he looked at the distance he still

had to travel and thought of giving up. But then he remembered that Grandmother was somewhere down below, waiting to talk to the Rabbi. He knew he had to find her and stop her. Not for himself. Not because of the shame he would feel when Jesus denounced him as a fraud, but because of Peter.

I would give anything to see Peter standing straight and tall, he thought, and he meant it.

The afternoon sun beat down on Aaron's head. He was drenched in sweat. His throat felt as if it was caked with sand. When he rested for a moment and tried to cough up the dust, a woman gave him a drink of water. As he returned the goatskin he saw for the first time that the palms of his hands were raw and bleeding. The backs of his bare legs were crisscrossed with scratches and scrapes. There was blood in the coating of dust. Every inch of the upper half of his body ached.

There was no time to worry about which part hurt the most. He wiped his hot face on his sleeve and went on his slow, painful way.

At long last, half way down the slope, Aaron saw a group of people from the village. They were seated directly below him. He spotted John, and then Mark. There was no sign of Peter and his family. At the front of the group, sitting closest to the rock, he saw Grandmother's small bent figure. Rachel and Mother were seated one on each side of her, with Mary next to Mother.

Aaron's heart leaped. He had found them! He sighed a deep sigh of relief. Between Aaron and Grandmother the crowd was its thickest, but at least he knew where she was. He wiped his bloodstained hands on his robe and rested his aching body for a moment.

Jesus had turned towards him, and Aaron listened to his words.

"And now I must leave you. I must proclaim the Good News of the Kingdom of God to the other towns too, because that is what I was sent to do."

Stunned by the realization that he was too late, Aaron watched Jesus step down from the rock.

Chapter Nineteen

There was a brief silence, then the crowd rose to its feet. On all sides, people embraced one another in peace and fellowship.

Aaron slumped back against the rock. Families all around him were gathering up their belongings and preparing to leave. One man stepped back onto Aaron's hand. Another person almost tripped over him. Still Aaron didn't move. He sat with his head bowed, aching with pain and disappointment.

A few people were walking towards the rock. A man staggered down the slope with a crippled girl on his back. Two boys led a wild-looking man at the end of a rope. The man lunged from side to side, chanting "Son of God! Son of God!" as he went by.

The bulk of the crowd headed up the slopes to go home. They were talking about what they had heard, and looking back at Jesus. They didn't see Aaron. As they pressed past him, dust rose in clouds from their feet.

"Don't panic," he told himself when he started

to choke. "Get up."

Using the rock and his staff, Aaron struggled to his feet. He leaned against the rock and wiped his streaming eyes on his sleeve. Through a sudden gap in the crowd he saw Grandmother. Mother and Rachel were helping her over the rough ground towards Jesus. Other people had reached him first. They were gathered around him, and he was speaking to each in turn.

Aaron tried to call to her, but his dust-lined throat swallowed the words.

I must reach her before it is too late! he thought.

He coughed and gasped for air and coughed again. He almost fell as somebody jostled him in passing. He regained his balance, and tried to judge the distance between himself and Jesus. It seemed impossibly far. If he tried to cover it in his usual way he knew he would be trampled underfoot. If he waited until the crowd thinned, he would be too late.

People surged past him, talking among themselves. They stumbled over rocks and slid on the loose soil and helped each other up and hurried on. Aaron stayed where he was, unable to decide what to do. Then, through another gap, he saw Grandmother again. It would soon be her turn to speak.

Shaking from head to foot, Aaron stepped away from the safety of the rock. He launched himself against the tide of humans. He staggered this way and that, jostled but held up by the good-natured crowd. A man appeared in front of him. He was carrying a child in his arms. He, too, was heading towards Jesus. Aaron lurched along in the gap the crowd made to let the man through. He held on to the back of the man's robe to keep his balance.

Aaron stopped when he reached the foot of the rise where Jesus was standing. The man moved on, leaving Aaron's fingers grasping at the air. Aaron swayed, and almost lost his balance.

"Stop Grandmother! Wait! Don't do it!"

It was meant to be a mighty shout, but it came out as a hoarse whisper. No one heard him. Aaron looked around. Where were John and Mark? Where were his neighbors from the village?

He threw himself up the incline, stumbling a few precious steps nearer. Some people had moved into his line of sight. He could no longer see Grandmother. Was she speaking to Jesus? Was she saying, "Please, Rabbi, cure my grandson Aaron . . . ."

"Please no! Don't do it," Aaron groaned.

He forced himself forward. His whole body throbbed with the effort. He tripped over a root and his staff slipped from his hands. As he lunged for it, it bounced out of reach. He lost his balance and fell to his knees. Exhausted and in pain he bent forward and rested his sweat-streaked face against a clump of grass.

After a moment, he felt a hand under his elbow. A stranger was helping him to his feet. The man handed Aaron his staff and was gone.

The group around Jesus had moved. Aaron had a clear view of Grandmother. She was just about to speak to Jesus. He was bending over her, taking her hands.

"Don't!" Aaron formed the word, but no sound

came out. As if in a dream, he watched his grandmother's lips move. He could hear her quavering voice, but her words were lost in the murmur of the people around her.

"Don't," he pleaded silently. "Ask for help for Peter, not for me. Ask for yourself."

It was at that moment, Jesus looked up. He stared over the top of Grandmother's head straight into Aaron's desperate eyes. Aaron froze. Over his thudding heart, he heard Jesus's answer. The calm, comforting voice carried easily to where Aaron stood, panting and afraid.

"Your grandson doesn't need my help, Mother. He has cured himself."

Once more the stranger's eyes met his. Aaron's heart leaped. Love was in that glance, and total understanding. It was the same kind of look Aaron's father had given him.

As Aaron puzzled over the Rabbi's words, he looked down at himself.

I am standing, he thought with astonishment. *I am standing with nothing but my staff to hold me up!*

"Aaron!" Mark was running towards him. "You walked! Did you see how far you walked?"

"What . . . . . ?" Aaron was too weary to understand.

"Look." Aaron followed Mark's pointing finger. "See that rock? You walked all the way from there without help. We were halfway up the hill before we saw you. Didn't you hear us calling you?"

"You walked, Aaron!" John was beside him. His strong arm was around Aaron's shoulders. Without it Aaron was sure he would have fallen.

The slopes were almost clear of people. The distance from the rock to where Aaron was standing seemed to be impossibly far.

"Did you hear what Jesus said?" John asked. "He *knew* Aaron, but he didn't condemn you. I could tell by the way he looked at you that he knew everything."

Aaron nodded. He looked to where Jesus was surrounded by people wanting his help. He felt a surge of joy like nothing he had ever felt before.

I am free, he thought. *Free to start all over again.*

Mother came hurrying up. She took his dirt-streaked face in her hands.

"You walked." She was crying and laughing at the same time. "Oh, Aaron, *look* at you."

Aaron's arms and legs were streaked with blood and dirt. His hands and elbows were raw, his robe was torn. He wiped the sweat from his face with his dusty sleeve, making it dirtier than ever.

Grandmother came slowly towards them. She was leaning on Rachel's arm.

"Aaron?" she cried. "You can walk again. Jesus says you are cured." Tears streamed from her cloudy eyes.

"Mary, give your brother the water bag," Mother ordered. "He needs a drink."

Aaron drank greedily. "There is something I must do," he said, as he returned the bag.

"Haven't you done enough for one day?" Grandmother asked. "You must rest, Aaron."

Aaron caught Mark's eye and they burst out laughing.

"Rest? I have been resting long enough," Aaron

said. He pulled himself free of John's arm. "I am going to ask Jesus to help Peter."

"Peter? Didn't you hear about Peter?" Rachel asked.

"Peter was . . . ." Mark said.

"Let me tell him," Rachel cried.

"Tell me what?"

"Peter is cured. He can walk." Rachel's eyes were glowing with delight. "It happened before Jesus started to preach. He walked past Peter and his family on his way down the slope. He stopped and looked at him and touched his legs. He told Peter to get up and walk and he did! Everybody saw it happen. It was wonderful, wasn't it, Mother?"

Mother nodded and sighed happily. "It has been a wonderful day."

"And what about Aaron?" Grandmother demanded. "I asked Jesus to cure Aaron and he did. I knew he would."

In the silence that followed, Aaron swallowed hard.

"No," he said slowly. "It was me. I . . ."

He felt a hand on his arm. Mother put her finger to her lips, and shook her head.

Aaron stepped forward and kissed his grandmother's cheek. "Thank you for what you did," he said.

She smiled her toothless smile at him, and held his arm. "Has the Rabbi gone?" she asked.

Aaron looked around. "He's gone," he said and felt a strange sense of longing.

Grandmother sighed. "Is there a rock nearby?" she asked. "I feel so tired. I will rest while somebody fetches my donkey. Mark, you and John had better take Aaron home. He has been very sick you know."

Mark grinned at Aaron's red face.

"Don't worry, Grandmother. I will look after him."

John was impatient to be off. He helped Grandmother over to a rock and said, "I'm going back to the flock. There is a lamb due to be born and I don't want to miss the birth. Father might need help."

"I'll go with you," Rachel said. "I want to tell Father how Peter was cured." She smiled at Aaron. "I will tell him about you, too, Aaron."

"He won't be surprised," Aaron said. "I went to see him first. Before I came here." He flushed and lowered his voice so Grandmother couldn't hear him. "I thought if I confessed everything, he would help me."

"And he refused," John said. "He said you had to do it yourself. Am I right?"

Aaron nodded. "He talked about me becoming a man. He said he had plans for me."

"He did have plans for you," John agreed. "He told me Uncle Mark had asked if you could go and live with him. He said Uncle Mark wanted to teach you his business. He thought you would be good at it. But that was when Father first came home."

"Live with Uncle Mark in Capernaum?" Aaron's mouth fell open. "Father said that?"

"He thought it was a good idea. Uncle Mark is lonely. It would be a good trade to learn. And he said having one of us in the market end of shepherding would be good for business." John shrugged. "Of course that was before he found out what you had done. I think you will have a long way to go before you can prove to him that you are worthy of his trust."

Aaron's head was whirling. So that was what Father meant by "plans." "When did Father think of sending me to live with Uncle Mark?" he asked.

"Next fleecing time. But he has changed his mind. If you can prove to him between now and then that you are serious and will work hard, maybe he will change it back again."

I will work harder than I have ever worked in my life, Aaron vowed to himself. *I will do anything he asks and I won't complain.*

"Are you able to walk back up the slope to where you left the donkey?" Mother asked. "If not, Mark can bring it down here."

"I'll walk," Aaron stuck out his chin. "If it takes me until nightfall I will do it. Then I am going to ride to Peter's house."

It was a long slow climb. Aaron had to stop and rest every few steps, but his legs held him up all the way. At the top he sat down while Mark fetched the donkeys. He had never felt so tired in all his life. But he felt happy too.

He could walk again, and he had something to look forward to.

"I will show Father what kind of man I will be," he said to himself. "I will work harder than anyone in the family."

He rested his head on his sore hands and stared down at the deserted slopes. Only trampled grass and crushed flowers showed where the huge crowd had been. The words of the Rabbi Jesus echoed in his head.

"Love your neighbor as yourself . . . . . Always treat others as you would have them treat you . . . . ."

The words gave him a wonderful warm feeling. His heart ached when he remembered he had missed the rest.

"I will ask Grandmother what he said," Aaron said to himself. "I know she will remember every word."

From where he was sitting, he could see for miles in every direction. He watched the streams of people heading towards their homes. He shaded his eyes and stared at the road to Capernaum.

Most of the people were so far away, they looked like ants. It was impossible to make out Jesus and his followers.

"What are you staring at, Aaron?" Mark was back with his donkey.

"I was looking for Jesus of Nazareth. I was wishing he hadn't gone. Do you think we will ever see him again?"

"I hope so," Mark said.

"I hope so, too," sighed Aaron.

the end